The Traveler's League: The Timepiece

Written by Nick Goss
Cover Design: TS95 Studios
Illustrations: Tara Faul
Editor: SJS Editorial Services

Published by Nicholas Goss, Nashville, TN
Copyright © 2018 Nicholas Goss

Publisher's Note: This is a work of fiction. Names, characters, places, and incidents are a product of the author's imagination. Locales and public names are sometimes used for atmospheric purposes.
 Any resemblance to actual people, living or dead, or to business, companies, events, institutions, or locales is completely coincidental.

Printed in the United States of America
ISBN 978-1-7321815-7-1 (Paperback)
ISBN 978-1-7321815-0-2 (EBook)

Note from the Author

Dear Reader,

I hope you enjoy reading this book as much as I enjoyed creating the story within it. The next story in this series is even better because of the feedback I receive from parents and children.

I highly value any and all feedback about my story, the writing, editing, artwork, etc. If you would please leave an honest review of this book, on the site from which you purchased it, it will help others make a more informed buying decision. And who knows? Maybe they and their kids will discover new worlds full of adventure and fantasy all because of your input!

With all of my heart, thank you for purchasing this book! Now let's get the adventure started...

~ Nick

Dedication

Homeschooling allowed me to unleash my creativity as a child. The mysteries of the natural world, romanticized thirst for adventure, and the belief that magic was somehow real, colored my school day.

Now, a child can't make his or her own decision to go down the homeschooling path, that's up to the parent to decide. I get that. And it's not for everybody. But it was perfect for me. And it was my mom who recognized that, and made the decision to let my imagination breath and my heart soar!

So, this first one is for you, Mom.

The Timepiece

Book 1 of The Traveler's League

By Nick Goss

Table of Contents

The Spell ....- 7 -

Strangers and Travelers ....- 11 -

Grounded ....- 17 -

Marooned ....- 24 -

Mirrors ....- 33 -

Burglars ....- 44 -

Shadow World..- 52 -

The Deep ....- 59 -

An Errand...- 64 -

Back to The Deep....................................- 73 -

Sirihbaz...- 84 -

Torpil...- 95 -

Animas ....- 104 -

The Feather ....- 115 -

Hapis..- 124 -

Escape...- 137 -

The Labyrinth ....- 147 -

Chamber of Crossroads..........................- 156 -

Traveler's Rest ....- 168 -

The Last Mission....................................- 180 -

"It's not an adventure until something goes wrong,"

-The Traveler's Code, Article I.

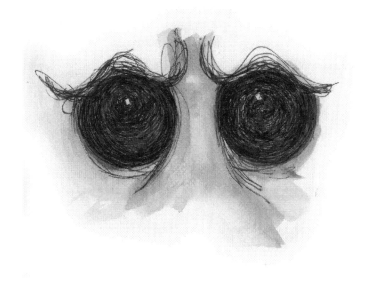

The Spell

Braxo held his blood-red dagger overhead. He had cast this spell a hundred times before, but something inside him said this time would be different. The Oracle moon had risen to its peak and was full again, allowing him to perform his dark work. With both hands on the handle of the knife, the black wizard closed his eyes and muttered the words to the spell. When he spoke the final word, he thrust the red blade into a giant block of dark crystal. A tiny deep-purple spark within flickered, and when he opened his eyes again, they were solid, black, inky orbs.

This spell allowed him to peek into the other worlds through the eyes of its creatures. He hunted, waited, and searched for the boy (it was always a boy) who traveled from world to world using the power of an item that Braxo desperately needed. The boy was always different, but the item was always the same—the timepiece.

Braxo looked at a jungle. He was in the mind of a great beast with a long snout like a crocodile, and from the tip of its nose grew a horn like a rhino. When Braxo took control of the creature's mind, it was drinking from a pool at the base of a waterfall. The spell always put him close to the timepiece, wherever it was, and each time he cast it, he became more skilled at getting closer.

The sound of a snapping twig or stick caught the creature's attention.

Braxo watched through its eyes as it scanned the opposite bank of the pool.

There! Across the pool was the shape of a young boy, frozen with fear at the sight of the beast. Braxo knew it was him—the traveler—the one who carried the timepiece.

He flooded the beast's mind with rage and commanded it to attack. As it jumped into the pool, Braxo whispered, "You're too late, boy. It's mine. Give it to me."

This boy was quicker than most and Braxo drove the creature down the jungle path after him with a fury. The beast bellowed from pain and fatigue just before slowing its pace, allowing the boy to get farther down the path, around a bend, and out of sight. Braxo waited a few moments for the beast to catch its breath, then doubled the rage he poured into its mind. It plodded on to the end of the path that spilled out onto a beach.

Bursting out of the jungle and onto the sand, Braxo saw the boy by the water's edge holding his precious timepiece. Golden streamers of magic dust swirled around him and the timepiece. Only a few seconds more and the boy would escape. Braxo hurled a full dose of hate and pain into the beast's mind, and it plowed through the sand. Tilting its head to the side, it closed the distance between the boy and its own giant form in seconds. It opened its jaws wide and snapped them shut around the boy, but only sand and salty air filled its mouth. The boy and the timepiece had vanished, escaping just in time. Braxo had failed. And while he had failed a hundred times before, this was the closest he'd ever come.

Releasing the creature's mind, he returned to his own body. Removing the dagger from the crystal, he called out to his servant.

"GeriPog!"

A small dwarven man about three feet tall waddled into the wizard's chamber.

"Yes, Lord?" GeriPog was dressed entirely in faded black, from his tiny cap, to his scuffed leather boots. His silver beard hung down to his knees, and his face and head were covered from the scars he'd earned from a life of slavery and abuse.

"Go to the forest outside the WolliPog village," Braxo ordered. "Hide yourself along the path and report back to me when he arrives. The boy is traveling."

Strangers and Travelers

The bell rang and a flood of kids burst out of Grandville Elementary and Middle School. It was that last bell they would hear until they came back after summer break. A tall ten-year-old boy adjusted his backpack and lumbered to a crosswalk, where a crossing guard halted traffic and led a group of kids safely across the street to the city park. The boy's bright blonde hair was unkempt. He didn't have a hat with his favorite sports team on it like the other boys. He didn't care much for sports anyways. His red collared shirt was plain, and his blue jeans were off-brand. He didn't wear designer clothes like the other kids, and his shoes were just plain old white tennis shoes. Hoops tried to act like none of that mattered and caught up to a group of boys from his class, and listened as they bragged about how they would spend their summer.

"We're flying down to Florida again. Going to Disney World. My little sister has never been, so..." one boy casually boasted.

"That's cool. We're going to Hawaii next month. I think my dad is going to take us scuba diving!" the other boy shared. "What about you, Hoops? What are you doing this summer?"

"My mom and I will probably just go down to Washington D.C. See the Capitol, meet the president, maybe fix the whole country. Nothing huge." They all laughed together.

"But seriously, what are you going to do?"

"I really don't know," Hoops lied. "My mom won't tell me."

The truth was Hoops' mom worked two jobs and didn't have extra money for vacations. It was all she could do to keep them in a nice part of town, near a good school. She was a great mom, but Hoops was embarrassed that they were poor. "I hope you guys have fun. Let me know when you get back so we can hang out before school starts."

Hoops hoped they'd come back soon, and they'd be the same. The last day of school is weird like that. Friends say goodbye, secretly hoping they'll still be friends when they meet again in the fall. They hope they won't have changed too much from the travels and adventures of summer.

When they got to the middle of the park, the boys all said goodbye to each other and went their own separate ways. Hoops was alone, but his apartment was on the other side of the park, just across the street. This was his favorite part of the day. He loved messing with the pigeons as they waddled around the big fountain in the center of the park. He stopped here to sit on his favorite bench while he daydreamed about a more exciting life.

Pulling out an extra corn dog he'd taken from school, he fed his feathered friends.

It was easy to lose track of time. And his mom would start worrying about him if he didn't get home by six thirty. So, after the pigeons were fed, he jumped up from the bench and headed home. Just then a boy's voice called out to him from behind.

"There you are! I've been looking all over for you." The boy was tall and skinny, with short, red hair. He was at least a couple of years older than Hoops.

"Who are you?" Hoops replied. "Do you go to my school or something?"

"No. You don't know me, but I know who you are. Well, kind of. I know who you *will* be." The boy smiled as he talked. "My name's Pete Smith... friends call me 'Smitty.'" The boy extended his hand for a handshake, and as he did, Hoops noticed a gold medal hanging from a red and white-striped ribbon. It was pinned to his shirt just above his left pocket.

Hoops' mom had warned him not to talk to strangers in the park, or anywhere for that matter. Even though this *Smitty* was a boy, he was an *older* boy, and he was still a stranger. "I'm not sure what you mean, but I've gotta get going. My mom will go nuts if I'm not home by six thirty. She's probably already looking for me."

"Ha!" Smitty shouted. "That's so funny. When you said six thirty, I knew I found the right kid. Look, I know that doesn't make sense yet, and this all sounds weird, but I have something I'd like to give you."

Out of his pocket, he pulled a small rolled-up piece of paper like a scroll, tied with a red ribbon and sealed with a blob of red wax. The wax seal had the letters 'T.L.' stamped on it. Smitty handed the scroll to Hoops.

"Don't break the seal and read the scroll until you get home," Smitty said.

"What is it? Some kind of coupon? Or like an invitation to a birthday party?"

Smitty smiled again. "It's the code. The Traveler's Code."

Hoops was still suspicious and a little scared, but he took the scroll anyway. "Thanks for the weird note, I guess…" Hoops said as he turned to walk away.

"Wait! I haven't given you the rest of it," Smitty said as he laughed. "This is the best part!" He reached in his other pocket and pulled out an old pocket watch. He opened it and set it to one o'clock and handed it to Hoops. "Don't wind it up until you get home. And read the Traveler's Code first."

Hoops reached out and took the timepiece and looked at it closely. Hoops tried to figure out why he was being given a gift by a strange boy.

"So... you're just giving it to me? Why?"

"Because I have to. It's my last mission." Smitty looked a little sad. "And it's chosen you to be next."

"Next?" Hoops was confused, curious, and excited all at once. "The next WHAT?" he said as he looked down at the timepiece in his hand.

"You're the next traveler!" said Smitty.

A thousand questions raced through his ten-year-old brain, but when Hoops looked up, Smitty was *gone.*

Grounded

"Where have you been?!" Hoops' mom was upset. "I've been worried sick about you. How many times have I told you to come straight home after school?"

"Sorry, Mom. I was trying to get home by six thirty, but I made a new friend at the park and I lost track of the time again."

Hoops' mom said, "Well, I'm glad you're okay, but it's no excuse. You're grounded for a week. NO friends. NO park. And NO going anywhere alone. Understand?"

"Yes, ma'am." Hoops said as he stared at the floor. He tried to look sad, but his hands were in his pockets, feeling the paper scroll and the timepiece. All that he could think about was going to his room and checking out the gifts Smitty had given him.

Hoops' mom sighed and said, "Who's this new friend? Does he go to your school?" But before he could answer, Mom glanced at her phone and sighed. "Shoot. I have go to work now. I'm running late." His mom gave him a quick hug and said, "Your dinner is on the table. Keep the door locked until I come home. If you need anything, you can call Ms. Grankel next door."

Ms. Grankel was the grouchy old lady next door. All she did was sit and watch TV, and occasionally knocked on the wall when Hoops was being too loud. She liked Hoops and his mom and was a good neighbor but didn't like the noise that ten-year-olds could sometimes make.

And her apartment was so boring! If he went over there for something, she'd sometimes ask him to keep her company. He'd just sit quietly on the couch while she watched stupid shows where people yell at each other. Instead, he would make sure he was quiet and didn't have to go over and ask her for anything. It was way better to just figure things out on his own.

His mom hurried out the front door. As soon as it shut, Hoops ran to his room like a rabbit with its butt on fire. He slammed his door shut and jumped onto his bed. He didn't even think about his dinner, or how hungry he was. He was too excited.

Bang. Bang. Bang. Ms. Grankel heard his door slam and knocked on the wall. "Sorry," he said in a loud voice.

He sat down on his bed with his legs crossed and emptied his pockets. Holding the scroll, he rolled it between his hands, then rubbed his fingers over the red wax. He broke the seal in half, and a big roll of thunder boomed outside. *Whoa. That was weird.* His heart raced as he unrolled the paper and read...

The Traveler's Code

I.   It's not an adventure
       'til something goes wrong.
II.   You can only be brave
       when you're scared.
III.   Through Four Gates and Five Worlds
       by watch or by song,
IV.   Your journey is meant to be shared.
V.   Adventures are wasted
       on those who don't learn.
VI.   Adventures must come to their ends.
VII.   But there's always another one
       'round the next curve.
VIII. And in Traveler's Rest,
       you'll find friends.
IX.   So, cheer up, young traveler,
       Adventure awaits!
X.   The timepiece has chosen you to roam.
XI.   And no matter the time
       or where you go next
XII.   At six thirty, you'll always come home.

When he was done reading the scroll, he read it again aloud. Then he read it again. He read it over and over until he could recite it with his eyes closed. As simple as the poem was, it was cryptic enough to make his ten-year-old brain buzz with questions. He hummed a tune that fit nicely to the words, so that it would be locked in his memory—a riddle wrapped in a song.

He examined the timepiece again. It was made of tarnished, faded copper and was heavy in his hand. Popping the lid open, he noticed it was still set to one o'clock. *Hmmm. The batteries must be dead. I wonder what kind of batteries it takes.* He flipped it over to find the cover for the batteries, but there were none. *What a curious antique. Things must have been so different in ancient times.* As he thought about how it was built and what could possibly make it run, he remembered what Smitty had told him, *"Don't **wind it up** until you get home and read the Traveler's Code first."*

"Duh," he said aloud as he turned the little winding knob at the top. He then held it to his ear and could hear the soft clicking of the gears inside. Click. Click. Click. Click.

A quick glance at the alarm clock by his bed told him the current time was seven fifteen p.m. He set the hands of the pocket watch to match his electric alarm clock, but as soon as he let go of the knob, the hands on the timepiece slowly slid back to one o'clock! He tried again. Same thing. The pocket watch kept resetting itself to one o'clock.

Hoops tried over and over again to set it to a different time, but each attempt ended in frustration. The pocket watch wouldn't work the way a normal clock *should*. He snapped the timepiece shut and tossed it on the bed in front of him.

"Stupid piece of junk!" he blurted. Just then, a crash of thunder pealed across the sky outside. It scared him, and he froze, staring at the timepiece for what seemed like several minutes.

When his heart stopped racing, he carefully took the pocket watch in his hand again. The lid was worn like an old nickel. The copper coloring had been rubbed away over who knows how much time, revealing a silvery base metal underneath. It had certainly been used a lot and needed a good polishing. So, he laid it in the palm of his hand and rubbed.

Particles of dust in the air glowed like tiny yellow stars and began moving in a big circle around Hoops. He kept rubbing and they swirled closer and faster around him. They crackled as they whooshed around him closer and closer until he was in a micro-tornado of swirling magic dust.

    Whoosh. The world vanished.

Marooned

Hoops opened his eyes to find himself sitting in yellow sand, staring at an ocean. He jumped up in a panic as he looked around. Where was his room? His apartment? Where was he and how will he get home? He knew he was in big trouble. The city he lived in was nowhere near an ocean. It was hundreds of miles away, in fact. His mom would freak out when she came home. *Maybe this is just a dream.*

He tried to make sense of what just happened. That whole 'swirl of magic dust thing' when he rubbed the watch was most exciting thing that had ever happened to him, and he was both scared and excited. The Traveler's Code came to mind and that first two lines made more sense now. *It's not an adventure 'til something goes wrong. You can only be brave when you're scared.* He was scared, that was for sure, and that alone seemed to confirm he was on an adventure!

Looking up, he saw the sky was light purple, but the sun was directly overhead. *A purple sky at noon? Weird.* Then his eyes opened wider than ever as he saw not one, but *two* crescent moons side by side just about to set over the ocean's horizon! Not only was he far away from his apartment and city, he was in an entirely new world! *I'm in BIG trouble.*

He reached down and picked the timepiece up and brushed off the yellow sand. He opened it to make sure it wasn't broken. It was still set to one o'clock but when he held it up to his ear, it wasn't clicking. He'd have to wind it up again, but after what just happened, you know, traveling to a new world and all, he wasn't quite ready to do that. This watch did something besides keep time. In fact, it didn't really keep time that well at all. Somehow, it helped him travel to this strange place.

This was the adventure he'd always dreamed of! Discovering a new world would make him the most legendary explorer in history. And he was only ten years old! He thought of his friends from school and how they were all bragging about what their families would be doing that summer: Disney World, Hawaii, amusement parks, and summer camps. *BORING*. This would be the best summer *ever* and he decided right then and there to begin exploring this strange place.

He turned his back to the water and looked at a jungle paradise in front of him. It was like a thick wall of trees and vines that went endlessly in both directions. He heard the loud noises of animals he didn't recognize, and saw things moving through the leaves and limbs above. The butterflies in his stomach told him he was a little scared, but he knew his adventure was somewhere in that jungle, or maybe it was the jungle itself. It was time to find out, so he began walking.

Everything changed once he was in the jungle. The trees above were so thick, there was less sunlight, and they blocked the cool wind from the beach. And since there was no wind, he could smell everything... and it was stinky. But dark, hot, and stinky wouldn't keep him from his adventure. So, he went deeper into the jungle.

He quickly found a path that he could follow. It was a trail that all the jungle creatures had worn down with use. He figured it must lead somewhere interesting so he followed it for a long time. Maybe a mile. Maybe two miles. He wasn't sure, and he didn't care. Eventually, the trail came to an end at the foot of an amazing waterfall. Bright blue water spilled down from hundreds of feet above, into a big pool that narrowed into a river on its other end. Hoops loved how the water would gush over the edge of the waterfall, then break apart into a wall of droplets, then transition to a curtain of mist at the bottom.

Where are all the animals? He could hear them when he first went into the jungle. He could surely smell them. He even used their path to get to the waterfall. Just then, as he scanned the opposite bank of the pool, he froze. On the other side of the pool, directly across from him, was an enormous creature. It was as big as an elephant, at least twice as tall as a grown man. It had leathery orange skin that had an eerie glow, making the jungle around it look darker. Each of its feet had three black claws and it had thick, dark-brown hair on its shoulders and running down the ridge of its back. Its neck was long like a horse, but its head made Hoops freeze with fear. It had jaws like a crocodile, with hair going from the top of its chin down its throat to its chest. It had two black horns shooting out the sides of its head that curved forward towards its snout and at the tip of its snout was a third horn like a rhino. It had wide, thick shoulders and chest and was smaller at its hips. Whatever it was, it was ugly, dangerous, and ill-tempered.

The creature snorted and gurgled as it licked up the water with its forked tongue. Its every move and sound seemed like a warning to all the other jungle creatures. Even as it would drink, it would snort and growl. Little birds would land on its back while it wasn't moving, so it would snort and growl. It didn't have a tail to swat the big flies away, so when they'd land on its back and bite, it would snort and growl.

Suddenly, the creature stretched its neck straight out, squeezed its eyes shut, and shivered. A huge fart ripped out of its backside; the force of the fart shook the bushes and leaves behind it. Tiny creatures scurried out of the bushes in a panic, and birds abandoned their hidden nests. The leaves turned orange and withered instantly. The beast snorted and growled. *That was the most toxic explosion of butt gas I've ever seen. The guys will never believe this!* He decided to name this new species the 'ridgeback toxigator,' but he didn't have a camera or a journal with him to make any notes. *I have to bring a camera with me next time. And what kind of explorer doesn't carry a journal?*

Another loud snort from the toxigator convinced Hoops it would be best to just leave the beast alone and head back to the beach. He backed away from the pool's edge very, very, VERY slowly, as silent as a ninja.

SNAP! Hoops stepped on a stick. *Oops.* He stopped and remained perfectly still as his heart raced. *Please don't see me. Please don't see me.* But the toxigator had excellent hearing and turned his head towards the sound across the pool. Its eyes were solid black, like two inky orbs with no pupils. And when they fell on Hoops, they filled with rage. *Oh no! It sees me!* The toxigator erupted in a blood-curdling, bone-chilling roar. It stomped its feet on the ground, and its whole body shivered with anger. It kicked the dirt out from behind its black-clawed legs and jumped into the pool towards Hoops.

A strange, loud, airy voice hissed through the trees all around him. "You're too late, boy. It's mine! Give it to me!" That was enough adventure for one day. Hoops turned and ran. His legs carried him faster than he'd ever gone in his life. He headed back the way he'd come along the path. As his heart pumped loudly in his ears, he could hear the toxigator in the jungle behind him. He could hear the snort, snort, snort, snort, with every gallop. He could hear the monster's feet thud, thud, thud, thud. And the sounds grew louder as the creature got closer. And that loud airy voice was terrifying! What was that? It came from everywhere all around him, and yet it came from the beast as well. "Give it to me, boy. It's mine! You can't escape."

Hoops kept going as fast as he could. He was in big trouble, and all he could think about as he ran was his mom, sitting at home worrying about him. Would he ever see her again? Would he die here? *No. I've got to get back home, but how?* The solution didn't come just then as it was hard to focus on a plan when a ridgeback toxigator charged at you in the middle of the jungle.

He was out of breath, but his legs kept moving him down the path. He would rather die from running out of breath than in the jaws of that stinky beast.

Then he noticed the toxigator's thuds and snorts were getting softer and slower. Hoops kept going anyway. *The beast must be getting tired and slowing down.* He glanced back to make sure, and yep! He was right! The beast had slowed down to a walk. It was still walking after him, but it was getting tired. When Hoops looked back, it bellowed out another loud, irritated roar. It still wanted him but couldn't catch him.

Hoops didn't stop running, nor did he slow down even a little bit. He thought about what would have happened if the toxigator had gotten a hold of him. Finally, he broke out of the jungle and onto the beach. The two crescent moons still hung over the horizon and he could see his footsteps from where he'd first started walking. He collapsed onto the soft cool sand and caught his breath. He was alive!

Catching his breath, he thought about the beast and the waterfall, the jungle path, and the watering pool. *A new world and a new species discovered by ME, the youngest and most daring explorer in history. Worthington D. Hooper.* If only he'd brought a camera, and a journal. What kind of adventurer doesn't take a camera and a journal? Another line from the Traveler's Code made sense. *Adventures are wasted on those who don't learn.*

He thought about returning to this world to recapture his discoveries. Perhaps next time, he would take a different path into the jungle, and maybe find a tree to climb up and observe from.

ROARRRRRRRRR... The beast was still in the jungle looking for him. And it was closer. Hoops stopped thinking about how great an explorer he was and focused on how to get home.

"Home," he whispered to himself. As he did, the final words of the Traveler's Code floated through his brain. *At six thirty, you'll always come home.* "Six thirty!" Hoops shouted at himself. Excitedly, he pulled out the timepiece, popped it open, and set the hands to six thirty. This time, the watch didn't reset itself. He wound it up, snapped it closed, and rubbed. The glowing sparks appeared and circled around him just as before. As the swirling electric particles surrounded him, the toxigator burst out of the jungle towards him. In a panic, he rubbed faster and faster. He desperately rubbed as the creature plowed through the sand, now only yards away. His heart pounded, and his arms grew stiff from fear. The tornado of sparks made it hard to see the hulking beast, now only a few feet from him. *Please hurry!* The beast lunged as it opened its mouth and wrapped its jaws around Hoops.

Whoosh! Everything went black.

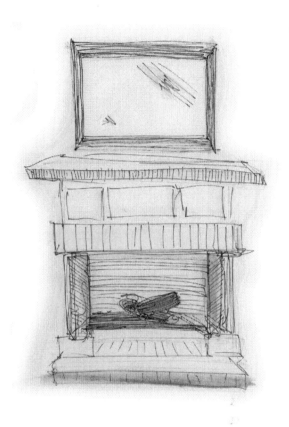

Mirrors

Hoops' room was just like he left it and the clock still said seven fifteen p.m. His bed felt extra soft and warm though, his legs ached from all the running, and his heart still beat quickly. Luckily, there was no ridgeback toxigator.

"Whew," he sighed to himself. His stomach growled, and he realized he should've eaten dinner before going on his adventure. He warmed up his food in the microwave, scarfed it all down like a wild animal, then went back to his room to get some sleep. He was exhausted.

When he pulled off his basketball shoes, yellow sand spilled out onto the carpet. The jungle beach had not been a dream and Hoops again felt silly for not taking a camera or a journal. *Well, at least I got a souvenir.*

Shutting his eyes, he thought about what his next adventure might be. He didn't seem to mind that he'd almost been eaten alive and lost in a strange world. He knew now there were more discoveries to make, worlds to explore, and daring adventures to experience. He pulled the Traveler's Code out of his pocket and read it again. *There's always another one 'round the next curve.* He was ready for more, but after some sleep.

When he awoke the next morning, he found himself face to face with King Tut, his pet mouse. Tut had gotten out of his cage again and had gone on his own little adventure, scampering around the house looking for crumbs. His little midnight mouse trips always ended by curling up beside Hoops' head. King Tut loved to snuggle up to Hoops' neck where it was nice and warm and safe.

"You better get back in your cage, your majesty. Mom's going to flip out if she sees you on my bed." Hoops' mom wasn't a King Tut fan as she didn't like rodents at all. But she had given the mouse to Hoops for his birthday last year because the pet was small, easy to take care of, and would keep Hoops company while she was at work. Hoops found King Tut to be his best friend and truest companion. Who needed a dog? King Tut was smart and could do all kinds of cool tricks. Also, he like to be petted.

"Squeak," said his majesty. He ran to the edge of the bed and made a huge leap off the covers onto the dresser. After sticking the landing, Tut scampered up the wall of the cage and dropped down through a hole in its lid that he had chewed open over time.

"Squeak?" he called when he was done.

"Yeah, sure. No problem, buddy." Hoops gave him a mouse treat before going to the kitchen for some breakfast. He could tell from his room that it was bacon and waffles, and the sound his stomach made told him it was time to chow down.

On his way to the kitchen, he passed through the living room. He glanced at himself in the huge mirror hanging over their gas fireplace and stopped to practice a couple of goofy faces. Then he tried his war face. "Bring it on," he told his reflection. Next he practiced his tough-guy face. "Are you talking to me, pal?" Then he went back to his goofball faces, then confused faces, then he stuck his tongue out and played air guitar like a rock star. "Rock on, bro," he said when he was done.

His mom hugged him and left for work while he finished his bacon and waffles. "Keep the door locked until I come home. If you need anything, you can call Ms. Grankel next door." She always said the exact same thing when she left.

"Okay. Bye, Mom."

When the door shut, he scarfed down the last piece of bacon, dashed to the living room, and plopped down in the big, brown, comfy chair by the fireplace. The chair faced the TV, and up until a couple of days ago that's how he'd prefer to pass the time, but now Hoops had zero interest in watching cartoons or doing anything at all except getting on with his next adventure.

He pulled the timepiece from his pocket, popped it open, and set it for two o'clock. "Let's do this!" he said as he wound it up. When he began rubbing, the magic glowing particles in the room came alive and rotated around him. Faster and faster, closer and closer. Just then, Hoops felt a cold little nose in his right ear.

"Squeak."

Whoosh! The living room vanished.

When Hoops opened his eyes, he said, "What are you doing, you crazy mouse? You can't go on this adventure. It's too dangerous. He reached up to his right shoulder to pet the mouse. But King Tut wasn't there. Then he felt Tut's cold nose on his *left* shoulder.

Hoops looked all around him, feeling both confused and disappointed. He reappeared in an apartment very similar to his own, and in the same building. His mind raced. *Did the timepiece not work the way it was supposed to? Where was the next world? The next adventure?* Looking around some more, he thought that maybe the pocket watch only made him travel across the hallway to his neighbor's apartment. It had the exact same size and layout, only reversed. But the chair Hoops sat in was his chair. The bookcase had *his* books on it but was now on the *left* side of the TV instead of the right. The fireplace was now on the *right* side of the chair but was supposed to be on the *left*.

Hoops jumped out of the chair and explored the apartment. The kitchen was just like his, only with everything backwards. There was even a plate of unfinished waffles on the table (minus the bacon). In *his* apartment, his bedroom was the one on the left side of the hallway, and his mom's was on the right. So, in this strange reverse apartment, he decided to check out the bedroom on the right. It was full of books (his books), but they all *had backwards letters on the covers and spines.* There was a mouse cage with a hole that had been chewed away in its lid on the desk. The bed was identical to his own *and there was yellow sand on the covers as well as the carpet!* There could be no doubt that this was his room, but he was getting dizzy from everything being opposite from where it normally was. After he'd lived somewhere for several years, he walked around corners and flipped light switches without thinking about it. But everything being in an opposite spot made Hoops feel woozy and confused.

Back in the living room, he leaned on the mantel of the fireplace. He thought if he looked in the big mirror so that everything would appear back to normal might help him calm down and get rid of the dizzy feeling. But things only got worse. He couldn't believe what he saw as he leaned on the mantel of the fireplace and peered into the mirror. To be more accurate, he couldn't believe what he DIDN'T see. Hoops had *no reflection.*

"Whoa!" Hoops hollered. The room in the mirror's image was back to normal, but oddly he couldn't see himself, King Tut, or the big brown comfy chair.

I think we're in the mirror!

Hoops suddenly froze as he watched (in the mirror) the front door open and his mom hurry back into the apartment. It was like watching her on TV. Turning around and away from the mirror, he watched her reflection as she walked right past him, mumbling something about keys as she went into the kitchen, digging through her purse.

I'm in a mirror dimension! This was a reflection world, and it mirrored his own. Whatever happened in the real-world dimension, which Hoops now called, "the six thirty world," controlled what he saw in the mirror world, *and he was actually there, in the mirror world.*

His mind burst with questions. What an amazing discovery! The first person to ever cross into another dimension... and he was only ten years old!

"Look out, history books," he told himself. "You're going to need a whole chapter devoted to the amazing accomplishments of Worthington D. Hooper. The greatest explorer of all time."

"Squeak," his majesty agreed that Hoops was amazing.

"Thanks, pal. You'll be the greatest mouse in world history, the close companion and loyal sidekick of the world's most outstanding adventurer mankind has ever known."

King Tut leapt off his shoulder onto the mantel. He put his tiny paws on the mirror and scratched. He obviously missed his own reflection.

"Me too," Hoops said. "It's weird not seeing my reflection. But if we're the originals, shouldn't we at least see a copy of ourselves around here somewhere?"

Hoops' brain hurt from trying to figure it all out and he still felt a little dizzy. He plopped down in the chair. "We must have replaced the reflections when we got here. That's probably why Mom didn't see us when she came home. We weren't actually there. We were here! INSIDE the mirror." Hoops thought his mom would have freaked out though, if she had looked in the mirror and saw Hoops standing next to her.

This was a very complicated world. It was too easy to make a mess of things. He was ready to get back to the six thirty world. "Let's go home."

As Hoops helped King Tut onto his shoulder, he looked at the TV. *I always wanted a TV in my room... I wonder...*

He unplugged the TV from the wall and carefully picked it up. He never knew they were so heavy! Setting it on the floor, he sat on top of it and pulled out the timepiece. He made sure his majesty was safely seated on his shoulder and set the pocket watch for six thirty. As he rubbed the watch, the swirl of magic glowing dust appeared and blocked his view of the reflection world. *This would be the perfect place to hide if I ever needed to.*

Whoosh! The reflection world vanished.

Hoops was back in his living room, with Tut on his shoulder and the TV from the mirror dimension under him. Everything was where it was supposed to be, and the words and letters on all the books were no longer backwards. He didn't feel woozy or confused anymore, and was relieved to no longer be in the mirror dimension. As he thought about how awesome it would be having an extra TV in the house (preferably in his room), his butt hit the floor.

"Ouch!"

The extra TV had vanished right out from under him! It had quickly dissolved into nothingness. It was just gone. Then Hoops saw something that freaked him out—the *other* TV disappeared too! The original. Then it was gone. Both TVs were gone.

This was a hard lesson to learn and he wasn't excited about this discovery at all, but he ran to his room and made an entry in his journal.

Two o'clock world - The Mirror Dimension. Rule #1: When the reflection of something crosses into the real world, our six thirty world, it must replace the original version. And if the original vanishes, so will the copy. NOTE: I've somehow lost my own reflection, and King Tut's. *I just destroyed our TV by bringing its reflection to the six thirty.*

Hoops knew he was in big, big trouble. How would he explain this to his mom? She would never believe him. He would no doubt be grounded for a month and forced to do all kinds of stupid chores to earn money for a new TV.

CRASH.

The sound of breaking glass made him jump. He spun around and looked at the mirror over the fireplace. It was fine, no breaks or cracks. Then he heard voices, grown men's voices. They were low, mean-sounding voices coming from the kitchen. He peeked around the corner into the kitchen to see two men dressed in jeans and black hoodies crawling through the kitchen window.

Burglars

Hoops ran to his room as quietly as he could and hid under his bed. His mom had talked about burglars before and he knew what to do, but he never thought he'd be this scared. He listened to the two men talking as they looked through the apartment. They made all kinds of noise as they opened drawers and turned things over. They were looking for anything valuable, and nothing in particular.

"What a dump," said the fat one. "You said this place would be perfect. I don't even think they have a TV."

"No, but it looks like it's just a lady and a kid that lives here. She's too busy to ever be here. And there are tons of people like that in this building." The skinny one was the boss. He was obviously tougher and meaner.

Hoops remembered that he was supposed to call the cops, but the cell phone was in the living room...

"Look!" said the fat one. "I gotta cell phone here. We can get a few bucks for that, at least."

"Shut up and look in the other rooms, Chubby," the skinny one ordered.

Hoops thought he might get caught. He knew that the fat one would mess up his room and most likely look under his bed. He needed to get out of there. He quietly slipped the timepiece out of his pocket again, wound it up, and rubbed. He didn't even take time to think about resetting it. He just rubbed quickly, and the timepiece did its job as always.

Whoosh!

The room was reversed again, and Hoops opened his eyes to see the fat face of the burglar peeking under the bed. He appeared to be looking right at Hoops but couldn't see him. Hoops still froze.

"This kid's got nothing. No computer. No video games. Just books and this pet mouse," Chubby reported. He left the room and Hoops crawled out from under the bed. He walked into the living room where the burglars grumbled and complained, looking through all his mom's stuff. Hoops was scared but he knew the burglars couldn't see or hear him. They were just the reflections of the six thirty burglars. And He was hiding from them in the reflection world.

He felt like a ghost.

The skinny burglar was getting irritated. The more irritated he got, the scarier he seemed. He reminded Hoops of the toxigator from the one o'clock jungle: an irritable, harsh, ugly, hateful beast. A beast who's just looking for his next meal, and ready to kill anything that threatened his territory.

"We're done here. Put that waffle DOWN, you fat tub of lard!" The fat one had decided to help himself to some of Hoops' leftover breakfast. "Let's go next door. I bet that old lady has got a bunch of jewelry."

Oh no. Ms. Grankel! Suddenly, Hoops wished he wasn't poor. He wished he had video games and a computer. He wished he had a TV. He wished he had anything the burglars wanted so they wouldn't go to Ms. Grankel's.

As the burglars opened the front door, Hoops followed. His mind raced. He tried to think of something, *anything* he could do to scare them away. When they got to Ms. Grankel's door, they didn't bother knocking. They used a crowbar and pried the door open and slipped inside.

Ms. Grankel was doing what she always did in the mornings. She was sitting in her rocking chair by her gas fireplace, rocking and watching some dumb show where people yell at each other. When the burglars rushed in, she had a terrified look on her face. She tried to get up, but the skinny burglar was quick. He walked over and put his hand on her shoulder and forced her back down into her chair.

"Try that again, Granny, and I'll kill you."

Hoops never felt hatred before. Fear, yes. Anger, of course. But when they *put their hands* on little old Ms. Grankel, he felt a burning, aching, raging hatred in his heart. He walked across the room and stood to the side of her fireplace while the crooks were busy looking around. Ms. Grankel's fireplace was just like Hoops' and it also had a big mirror hanging over it. All the apartments in their building did.

He waited for his moment. Just as the fat one got close to the fireplace, Hoops turned his back to the room and jumped in front of the mirror. The fat burglar in the six thirty saw Hoops in the mirror and he yelped like a dog, "Ah! Look. Look!"

As the skinny burglar came over to the mirror. Hoops made his meanest, maddest war face. He gritted his teeth and glared at the burglars with raging anger in his eyes.

The skinny one just stared at the mirror in disbelief. He was stunned but not terrified. The fat one peed his big, fat pants. Hoops could smell it.

"A... a... a... g... g... g... g...*ghost,*" the fat burglar said to no one in particular. "I'm leavin'. This ain't worth it."

Just as he was leaving, the skinny burglar became more angry than scared. "You ain't goin nowhere, Chubby!" He pulled out a gun and pointed it at his fat partner. "We're gonna finish the job." Then he turned and looked at Ms. Grankel. "Then we're gonna get rid of this old lady." He turned and looked in the mirror, *right into Hoops' eyes, smiled,* and said, "Enjoy the show, kid."

Hoops watched Chubby fill his little sack with Ms. Grankel's jewelry then waddle back into the living room. He was extra careful not to look in the mirror when he came back. He wasn't a fan of ghost children that lived in mirrors.

The skinny one wasn't afraid. Or at least he didn't act like it. He turned to the mirror and said, "You spooked the wrong guys, kid. Now granny's gonna join you in the afterlife." He pointed his big black revolver right at Ms. Grankel's head.

There was so much fear, hate, and anger in Hoop's heart, tears welled up in his eyes. Or maybe it was sorrow for getting sweet old Ms. Grankel into this mess.

He pulled out the watch and set it for six thirty. As the skinny burglar cocked the hammer of the revolver, Hoops furiously rubbed. Just as the swirls moved quickly around him, he reached out and grabbed the skinny burglar's *reflection* by the wrist.

Whoosh!

Hoops didn't open his eyes. He knew he had crossed back over into the six thirty world, but he didn't want to watch the burglar dissolve into nothing. But he could hear Chubby screaming. The fat burglar saw his skinny partner's reflection appear right next to him... with the little ghost boy holding his wrist. Then both the skinny burglar and his copy dissolved into nothingness from top to bottom in seconds.

"Please don't hurt me!" Chubby begged. "I'll do anything you want. Here! Take it all back." He tossed his little sack to Hoops' feet. All of Ms. Grankel's jewels fell out, and Hoops' cell phone.

Hoops picked up his phone and called the cops. When he was done, he told Chubby, "Your partner got what he deserved. Now you're going to jail. And when you get there, you can tell all your crook friends that the Ghost of Worthington will be watching them from the mirrors and waiting to take them away when they try to hurt people."

After the police took Chubby away, Hoops turned to Ms. Grankel to try to explain. "I'm sorry, Ms. Grankel. I know you're probably scared and don't know how all this is happening..."

"How long have you had the timepiece?" she interrupted.

"You know about the timepiece?!" Hoops was stunned. What does a little old lady know about adventure? Or other worlds? Or mirror dimensions?

"Young man, us old folks know quite a bit more than you realize," she said, smiling. "My daughter was a traveler a long time ago. I didn't believe any of her stories about the adventures she had at the time. But then something terrible happened. She took a friend with her to another world. A boy. I caught them playing with the pocket watch just before they vanished. Moments later, she returned. But the boy didn't." Ms. Grankel looked very sad thinking about it. "It doesn't matter now. What *does* matter is that you're safe. And I'm safe too, because of your bravery. Worthington D. Hooper, you are my hero." she said with the sweetest smile he'd ever seen. "You'd better get home. I have a feeling your adventures are just getting started. And there is still a lot of good work for you to do."

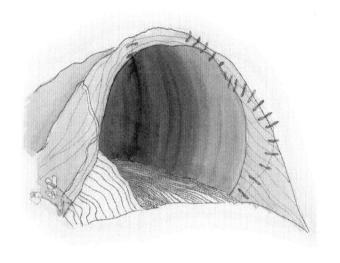

Shadow World

Hoops left Ms. Grankel's apartment feeling warmed inside by his new friendship, and an eagerness to continue into the timepiece's next mysterious world. When he got back to his room, he took

King Tut out of his cage and set him gently on his shoulder. He yanked the timepiece out of his pocket and set it to three o'clock. As he rubbed the lid, the electric glowing particles swirled around him. They moved faster and faster, closer and closer.

Whoosh! Everything went dark, like someone turned off all the lights.

Hoops opened his eyes, but everything was still totally dark. He rubbed his eyes and looked again. Same thing. Just sitting in the dark. He reached up to his shoulder and felt King Tut snuggling close to his neck.

"Whew. I'm glad you're still with me, buddy."

"Squeak." Tut jumped off his shoulder and scampered around. Mice can see in the dark, and Hoops knew this, so he wasn't afraid.

"I guess you'll need to be my eyes, your majesty. Lead the way!"

"Squeak." King Tut moved through the darkness so Hoops walked in the direction of his mousey little squeaks. Every few seconds, he would hear the mouse squeak and follow the sound.

Hoops heard Tut to his right, so he turned and could barely see something. It was a huge opening with the night sky in the distance. As Hoops walked through the opening, he realized he had been in a dark cave. As he came out, he looked up to see a dark-blue night sky with stars and constellations he'd never seen in any of his books.

The ground was rocky and sandy, and Hoops saw dead wood laying here and there. Turning around to look back at the cave, he discovered it was at the bottom of a giant rock wall. He was at the bottom of an enormous canyon. And it was darker than anyplace he'd ever been. The only light came from the stars. He plopped down on the dirt, crossed his legs, and thought.

King Tut crawled up on his knee and then jumped onto his shoulder again. He curled up by Hoops' neck and shivered.

"I know, buddy. It's so cold here." He wished he had brought a jacket, or a blanket. As he looked around, he saw all the dead, dry sticks laying around him. "I know! We'll go home and get some matches and build a fire! And I'll grab a flashlight, too, so we can take a good look at that cave."

He pulled out the pocket watch and rubbed it. He went back to the six thirty and sat on his bed when he opened his eyes. He ran to the kitchen and grabbed a big box of matches and a flashlight. He checked to make sure it worked, then grabbed a little hand mirror from his mom's dresser with all her makeup stuff.

"That way I can watch my back while I'm exploring that cave." He dumped his schoolbooks out of his backpack and put all his exploring supplies inside.

He also ate a sandwich and grabbed a handful of mouse treats for his majesty. Then he skipped back to his room, set the timepiece for three o'clock, and vanished back to the shadow world.

When everything went dark, he knew he was back in the cave. He pulled out the flashlight and hit the button... Nothing. Giving it a couple of shakes, he clicked the button a few more times but the darn thing wouldn't turn on. *Dang it.*

Once more, he relied on King Tut to guide him out of the cave with his little squeaks. Once he was out of the cave, he gathered a big pile of dead wood and placed a ring of rocks around it. Striking a match, he took a quick look around at the cold grey sand and the rocky opening of the cave. It was strange; that tiny flame seemed extra bright in this shadowy black place, as if a flame hadn't been seen in this world for hundreds of years. The flame burned close to his fingers, so he quickly placed the match under the pile of dead wood and it ignited without any problems. The flames chased away the cold instantly, and the crackling fire lit the ground all around it.

Hoops laid his backpack against the rock wall by the cave entrance and pulled out the mirror. He propped the mirror against the wall so he could see behind him and plopped on the ground again.

The fire blazed now but it wasn't too hot. In a way, he felt like he was camping out under the stars and wasn't afraid of being alone here. It was lifeless in this world. Nothing could survive here. It was just a dry, cold, dark, empty desert. And while loneliness was what he thought someone should feel in a barren place like this, he certainly *didn't* feel alone.

"I'm glad you're with me, your majesty," he said to the little white mouse curled up on the ground in front of the fire.

"I brought you some treats! Are you hungry?" He made the sign for treat and King Tut jumped up.

"Squeak!"

He tossed some treats here and there and King Tut would sniff around until he found them, then squeak again. Hoops tossed one over the fire. His majesty ran around the fire and munched on the treat.

The mouse was between the fire and the canyon wall, and as he munched on his little treat, Hoops froze. He couldn't believe his eyes. The light from the fire made not one, but TWO shadows of the mouse! The shadows were side by side, black and huge against the canyon wall.

"So, you lost your reflection, but you got an extra shadow!" Hoops told his majesty.

"Squeak," agreed the mouse.

He needed to write this down, so yanked his journal from the backpack and made an entry.

> Three o'clock world - The Shadow Realm. Rule #1: Light creates TWO shadows here! The world is covered in darkness and appears to be nothing but a desert.

Hoops pondered the strange discovery and tossed another treat to Tut. This one landed right in front of the mirror. The mouse scurried over to the treat. As he did, one of his two shadows passed over the mirror. And Hoops saw something he never thought he'd see again—the reflection of his little mouse! *The extra shadow created a new reflection! Another amazing discovery for the journal.*

> Three o'clock world - The Shadow Realm. Rule #2: The reflection of a second shadow creates a new reflection! Amazing!

He jumped up, more excited than ever, and stood between the fire and the canyon wall. His own big black twin shadows followed his every move. Stepping sideways to the right, he made one of his shadows pass in front of the mirror. The reflection of his face looked back at him from the mirror, smiling from ear to ear. What a relief! And what an amazing discovery!

Three o'clock world - The Shadow Realm. Note: I used the additional shadow to restore my own reflection!

Satisfied by all his new discoveries, he packed up all his stuff and placed King Tut on his shoulder. He decided to let the fire keep burning. Setting the timepiece to six thirty, he rubbed it and crossed back to his home world.

When his eyes opened, he jumped off his bed and with a heart full of hope, he dashed like a bolt of lightning into the living room. Facing the fireplace, he gazed into the mirror and laughed.

His reflection had been restored.

The Deep

Hoops felt invincible. He learned the secrets of other dimensions, logged his discoveries, recovered his shadow, and even saved Ms. Grankel's life. He told himself he was ready for anything and looked forward to romping through the next nine worlds.

When he awoke the next morning, his mom made him breakfast again and left for work. Again, Hoops found himself alone in his apartment. She had grounded him, fair and square, and he had to stay inside and wait another five days before his mom would let him enjoy the beginning of summer. It wasn't much of a punishment, though. It was more like his mom gave him permission to lock himself in his room and travel to strange new worlds.

Each world he explored seemed to be more interesting than the one before and he was ready to see whatever waited for him in the next. Grabbing the timepiece and setting it to four o'clock, he wound it up and snapped the lid shut. He rubbed and the micro-tornado of magic dust appeared.

Whoosh!

A wet chill swept over Hoops' body as he appeared in the new world *underwater*. The world around him was light hazy blue and he was floating. He couldn't breathe, and his eyes stung from the salt in the water. He was at the bottom of an ocean.

He should've held his breath when he rubbed the pocket watch. Looking up, he couldn't quite make out how far up the surface was. Just then, the timepiece slipped out of his hand and fell to the ocean floor! His lungs hurt, and he had to decide. If he swam up to the surface, there would be no way to hold his breath long enough to go back down to the ocean floor and find the timepiece. If he swam down after the timepiece, he would only have one chance to grab it, or he would drown.

With his lungs aching, he no longer felt invincible. His only chance to survive was to use the timepiece. He swam down.

Though his eyes burned from the salt water, he kept them open. He swam very quickly to the murky bottom of the sea. Long stalks of slimy seaweed grew out of it. He was so scared; he couldn't see the timepiece as he dug through the plants and sand. The more he dug, the more the sand kept clouding his vision.

He panicked. And the more he panicked, the cloudier the ocean floor became. He tried to calm himself, but it was too hard. He was about to pass out and his lungs felt like they were on fire. Just then, his hands brushed across the smooth metal of the pocket watch, which he quickly grabbed and set to six thirty. As he rubbed, he felt like it still might be too late. Any moment he would pass out, open his mouth, and breathe in the water, killing him instantly. *Just one more second.*

Whoosh!

Hoops opened his mouth, expecting his lungs to fill with ocean water and drown. Instead, the air of his bedroom rushed into him and he spent the next minute breathing heavily. A minute later, Hoops fell asleep. Exhausted from almost dying, he slept hard and he had strange dreams about underwater burglars and shadow toxigators.

He finally awoke at noon and glanced at his alarm clock. He wondered if he had just stayed in bed all morning and only dreamed of the underwater world. But his clothes and body were soaking wet. And the covers on the bed were wet too and smelled salty and fishy. He changed his clothes and pulled long stalks of stinky seaweed out of his pockets. Not thinking, he threw them in the kitchen trash can, causing the whole apartment to stink like a dirty beach.

Hoops was surprised that he had appeared underwater. That was unexpected, and certainly noteworthy.

Four o'clock world - The Deep. Rule #1: An entire world under the ocean surface. Without the proper gear, it's impossible to explore. NOTE: Next time, leave from the bathtub.

He was glad that he had forgotten to take King Tut with him this time! The poor little mouse wouldn't have made it back. His majesty would have been fish food for sure. At the same time, he was irritated that he didn't get to explore that watery new world. He resolved to go back, but next time, he'd be ready.

An Errand

The Traveler's Code stated that *Adventures are wasted on those who don't learn,* and Hoops needed to be prepared for the underwater world by gearing up, resting up, and having some way of documenting anything he might discover.

He cracked open his piggy bank and shoved all the bills and coins into his pockets. When he walked, he jingled and his pockets were stuffed so full they looked like a chipmunk's cheeks. Locking the front door behind him, he went outside to the front of the apartment building and got in a taxi.

"Scuba Stan's Dive Shop, please," he told the driver. The taxi took off while Hoops counted his money in the backseat. Forty-eight dollars and sixty-two cents! Surely that would be enough.

When he arrived at Scuba Stan's, he paid the cab driver, but it cost twenty dollars for the ride! That was almost half of everything he had. Things were so expensive in the city and he didn't really know why. *It's no wonder Mom must work all the time.* Just then, he realized he had been thinking about his next adventure so much, he forgot he was grounded.

Oh no. Mom's going to freak out. I'm toast.

The taxi driver waited while Hoops went into the dive shop. Scuba Stan had everything you could imagine: wet suits of every size and design, scuba masks, snorkels, flippers, harpoons, air tanks, and underwater cameras.

"Can I help you, kid?" said Scuba Stan.

"I need a scuba suit and enough air to last four hours underwater." Hoops tried to sound grown up.

Scuba Stan said, "How many days do you want to rent it?"

"Just for this afternoon, sir," Hoops confessed. He hoped it would be cheaper to only rent the gear for a few hours.

"Okay, kid. I think I have something in your size. Hang on a sec." Scuba Stan disappeared behind a curtain for a minute then came back with his arms full of underwater adventure gear.

"That will be sixty bucks, kid."

"Sixty dollars?! I'm only gonna be gone for like, three hours!" Hoops was angry at himself for blowing twenty dollars on a taxi ride, all for nothing.

"How much do you have?" said Scuba Stan.

"Twenty-eight dollars and sixty-two cents." Hoops was embarrassed.

"Well, that's not enough for the scuba suit, but is there anything else you're interested in?" Stan was a nice man. "What about an underwater camera? You can buy it for twenty bucks."

He would absolutely need an underwater camera because journals didn't work underwater. Hoops said, "I'll take it."

He ran outside with his new totally amazing camera to where the taxi driver still waited for him.

"You ready to go back home, kid?"

Hoops confessed he only had eight dollars and change and asked the driver if that would be enough to get him home.

"Not a chance." Grumbled the taxi driver as he drove off to find some paying customers.

It was a long walk home. Hoops knew how to get back home and wasn't scared of the city. He was scared of his mom. If he didn't make it home before she got off work, he'd be grounded for the rest of his life!

As he ran, he tried to think of some way to get his hands on enough money to rent the scuba gear. After all, a shortage of money was the main problem. An amazing idea flashed into his mind. It was so obvious that he stopped running and said aloud, "I wonder if I can create a new reflection of the money in the shadow world then bring it back from the mirror dimension without destroying it?" It felt like a long shot, but with the mysterious workings of the strange new dimensions, he sensed there might be a way. And he wouldn't give up until he figured it out.

He got home just before his mom did and waited for her to go to bed. Once she was asleep, he went to his room. He checked to make sure his eight remaining dollars were still in his pocket. He pulled out the timepiece and set it for three o'clock. Without hesitation, he wound it and rubbed the lid.

Whoosh!

Once again, he was deep in the shadow world cave again. This time, it was easy to find the opening. The fire he had started during his first visit still blazed and the glow could be seen from deep in the cave. Once Hoops got outside the entrance, he laid the hand mirror against the wall and put the money in front of it. The light from the fire created two shadows of the money. He moved his mom's hand mirror in front of both shadows and was pleased to see two stacks of money in the reflection! Setting the pocket watch to six thirty, he wished, "I hope this works," as glowing particles in the air swirled around him again. His visit to the shadow world was so brief and hurried, he failed to notice the strange images and writings on the cave wall.

Whoosh!

Back in his room, he pulled out his money again and peeked out his door to make sure his mom wasn't sitting in the living room. Even though she just went to bed, she often had problems sleeping through the night. She worked way too hard.

Tip-toeing into the living room, he walked up to the mirror above the fireplace. His reflection followed his every move and he was so happy to see his own face again. Carefully, he placed the stack of eight one-dollar bills on the mantel and saw in the mirror's reflection two stacks of bills, side by side! Hoops was so excited he could barely keep quiet. He had just used the timepiece and its worlds to double his money.

Thinking through his next move, he knew he couldn't move a reflection from the mirror dimension back to the six thirty world. That would destroy both the reflection of the money and the original stack of bills, just like the TV. The only thing he could think to try, was to move a reflection from the mirror dimension directly into the shadow world first, and from there, move it to the six thirty. It was hard to keep track of all the steps. *This is getting crazy. I'm going to make a big mess of things if I'm not careful.* But it was worth trying and he was determined to continue his travels to the underwater world. He thought that adventures would always just happen, and never considered that he'd have to work hard at preparing for them.

Setting the timepiece for two o'clock, Hoops realized that if he made this trip back to the mirror world, he would lose his reflection again. He didn't like that idea at all, and he almost considered giving up on this errand. He loved his reflection and the feeling of not seeing it when he looked in the mirror was a very unnerving one. Still, he was familiar with the rules of the shadow and mirror worlds and his experience had taught him he could get his reflection back, following certain steps.

Rubbing the timepiece, he gave his reflection a wink and a smile, and said "Sorry, buddy. I gotta do this. I'll bring you back when my mission is complete."

Whoosh!

The reversed surroundings of the two o'clock world made him feel confused and woozy again. But luckily, the extra money he'd created was easily transported from there, back to the shadow world. The dark three o'clock realm was the perfect back door for reflections entering the six thirty! When the reflections of Hoops' stacks of bills were whisked from the shadow world to his bedroom in the six thirty, they didn't dissolve into nothingness. Nor was the original money destroyed. This was the perfect loophole!

Three o'clock world - The Shadow Realm. Rule #3: You can move reflections from the mirror world into the shadow realm safely.

From there, you can move the reflection directly into the six thirty without destroying the original or the copy. NOTE: I just created double money! But I have to go back and get my reflection restored at some point.

He spent the next two days going through the three worlds in a circuit. Over and over and over again, each time doubling the total amount of bills. It wasn't an adventure at all. It was boring, repetitive work. But Hoops knew it was worth it. It meant he could get on with his exploration of the underwater world. And having all that money also meant his mom wouldn't have to work so hard all the time. Of course, he wouldn't tell her that until after he'd explored all the worlds the pocket watch had to offer. He had too many discoveries to make first. There was just so much to do and see, and now he had the money to do it right.

After the two days of hard work copying and doubling his money, he took a taxi back to Scuba Stan's Dive Shop. He rented all the needed equipment, and some extra film for his underwater camera. When he got home, he ate as much dinner as he could, knowing that swimming made a person hungry. He knew he would need as much energy as possible, so he told his mom he was going to bed early.

"Are you feeling okay, Worthington?" His mom felt his forehead for a fever. She thought he might be getting sick. What ten-year-old boy wants to go to bed early?

"Yeah. I'm fine. I just want the week to be over so I'm not grounded anymore. I figure the sooner I go to bed, the sooner the next day will get here." That's the type of thing he knew his mom liked to hear him say. And it was the truth, but it wasn't the whole truth.

Back to The Deep

Hoops heard his mom say goodbye again as she left for work the next morning. He was already done putting his scuba suit on and worked on getting the oxygen tank comfortably situated on his back. Once complete, he double and triple checked each piece of gear to make sure it worked properly. Putting on his flippers next, he waddled like a penguin into the bathroom. He climbed into the tub and put his mask on, taking several breaths of air to make sure he would be able to breathe. He set the timepiece to four o' clock and held it in his left hand, while he held his new underwater camera in his right. Even though his air tank and mask worked perfectly, when he rubbed the timepiece, he still couldn't help holding his breath.

Whoosh!

Hoops opened his eyes and found himself in a sparkling turquoise world. He could see clearly in his scuba goggles and his heart raced as he took in the dazzling underwater environment. In every direction, the sight of the ocean world was more beautiful than anything he'd ever imagined. Only when his lungs started to burn did he realize he was still holding his breath. So, clutching the timepiece in his hand, just in case, he took a good breath and filled his lungs with air. The scuba apparatus did its job and he could breathe quite normally. Several more deep full breaths helped to calm him and to get used to using the mouthpiece. Then it was time to explore.

Hoops swam downward and slowly skimmed above the ocean floor at about twenty feet. Seaweed covered the sandy ocean bottom in little grassy pockets. Each patch grew between massive coral formations, whose top surfaces played host to countless new species of fish, eel, and crustacean.

Hoops set to work using his new underwater camera. With every picture, he grew more and more excited. Each creature documented was a new discovery, a new species. And he was the one to first lay human eyes on it. Worthington D. Hooper, the youngest and most daring underwater explorer in history.

He spent over three hours snapping pictures of new species of fish. There was so much to take in and he needed more time than he had air in his oxygen tank to do it. But he still had about an hour's worth of air left, so keeping a close eye on his air levels, he decided to take a break from the photos and explore the coral formations. Down to the sandy bottom he swam. The light-green seaweed went all the way up to his waist when he put his flippers down on the ocean floor and stood straight. He felt a little tickle of fear in his stomach, knowing that anything hiding in here could sneak up on him easily. This awareness made him move very slowly with eyes wide open for any signs of danger.

The little pasture of seaweed stretched in several directions between coral formations. One gap between these coral mounds was bigger than the others and through it, the water was darker. That meant open ocean and deeper water to explore. Hoops slowly flippered his way through the opening, noticing the seaweed covering the floor stopped at a ledge. It took him a minute to take in the sight of an enormous underwater crater. It was as big across as a football field and about fifty feet deep. The floor of the crater was bare, just shells and rocks and sand. On the opposite end of the crater, in the wall near the bottom was a cave.

Hoops feared nothing anymore. He had grown over-confident in his ability to figure things out and reasoned that the pocket watch was a free ticket to escape danger anytime he needed it. So, he flippered his way to the mouth of this cave, which was at least twice as tall as him. The cave ran like a tube, straight back about a hundred feet before it curved to the right. There was a pale red glow coming from around that curve and it would grow slightly brighter then dimmer, brighter then dimmer. With it, a rumbling bubbling sound matched the slow steady rhythm of the light's waxing and waning.

Hoops burst with excitement to see what was around that curve and had his camera ready. He swam straight down that cave to the back and peeked around that corner.

The cave opened into a large round chamber. Hoops could feel that the water was a lot warmer here, almost hot in fact. The room was filled with the oscillating pale red glow and the rumbling bubbling sound bounced off the walls, creating a chant-like melody. And in the very center of this room lay the beast.

Once again stunned by a new discovery, Hoops almost forgot to breathe. He could barely believe his eyes. He couldn't identify what species it was, but from all the oceanic books and pictures he'd studied, it appeared to be some terrifying hodgepodge aqua predators. Its length was that of a small whale, but its form was too strange for our world. It was blobby all over, with smooth green-grey skin. It didn't have scales. Its head was like a deformed hammerhead shark, but with the protruding jaw structure and teeth of a Great White. From its forehead extended an antenna from which dangled a basketball-sized sac filled with red chemicals that emitted the pale light filing the chamber. The water around the glowing sac would boil from its heat, producing the rumbling bubbling sound. The bubbles produce from the boiling floated to the ceiling and escaped through tiny holes in the coral above. No, it wasn't a whale. It wasn't a shark either. It didn't have a tail. It had five long, fat tentacles, like the bodies of eels. The tentacles were wrapped around a small nest dug in the sand and in the nest were a dozen slightly misshapen oval eggs. They were planted upright in a tight cluster and each was the size of a football.

This strange creature was asleep, snoring, and cradling her eggs. Terrifying as it was to look at, Hoops felt privileged to see it up close, and not behind the glass of an aquarium. He appreciated the beautiful ugliness of this newly discovered creature, blobbiness and all, and felt like the respectful thing to do would be to take a quick picture, then swim quietly away to let this mother rest with her babies. He pulled out his camera and snapped a quick photo.

FLASH!

Oh no! I forgot to turn off the flash! Hoops gasped.

The monster stirred, and the pulsing light from the antenna froze. Hoops didn't bother to see what happened next. He turned in a panic and swam down the tube to the entrance of the cave. Behind him, he heard a low, violent rush of water, and a guttural scrapy moan. When he got to the mouth of the cave, he turned to look behind him. The creature's head emerged from around the corner. Her glazy red eyes caught sight of him and she lurched into the tube. The chase was on!

Hoops didn't swim to the center of the crater because he didn't want to be out in the open. Instead, he swam straight up the crater wall above the cave entrance. Halfway up, he looked below his feet to see the creature emerge from the mouth of the cave and out into the crater. It skimmed the ocean floor, darting this way and that, looking for the intruder. It would lurch with its powerful tentacles and glide in wide circles. The sound of Hoops' clumsy rushed flippers pounding the water drew the monster's attention upward and with another menacing moan, it lurched in his direction. Almost at the top, he saw a tiny crevice between two coral formations and swam for his life. He panicked as he pounded through the water. The timepiece slipped out of his hand as he used his arms to try to swim faster. It sunk to the bottom of the crater, and he had no time or interest in turning around to get it. He heard the gurgling rushing of the sea beast behind him, but he didn't look back. It was so close he could feel the heat from its antenna sac on his legs.

With one final kick of his flippers, he made it to the crevice and squeezed himself between the coral blocks. The monster slammed into the coral and stopped only inches away from his feet. He didn't notice the cuts and scrapes he had given himself scrambling between the coral. His stomach felt like it was tied up in knots. It hurt from all the fear and excitement. The monster gnashed and pushed against the coral, each time grinding off little pieces. The opening grew bigger and bigger, and with only a few more smashes, the creature could squeeze in and reach Hoops. He was fish food, for sure! The glazy red eyes of the monster, filled with fury, were only a foot away from him. Hoops was so terrified that he 'released his bowels,' that is, he peed in his scuba suit. As he did, his stomach untied itself and a rush of gas shot through his intestines and out his butt.

The bubbles of his underwater fart shot out into the face of the beast. As the bubbles popped around the beast's glowing antenna sac, it turned bright red and suddenly burst open! The creature twitched and wriggled violently for a few seconds, then went completely still.

It was dead. The chemicals from the sac warmed the water around Hoops and he used his flippers to push it away from him by its head. The eyes had turned cloudy grey. No life at all.

Hoops lost no time and dove to the bottom of the crater and retrieved the timepiece. Checking his oxygen meter on his wrist, he saw that he only had a few more minutes of air left. He decided to make the best of it. He tied the pocket watch to his scuba suit and swam back up to the dead beast. As he took out his camera and flashed away, the dead carcass of the sea beast did what all dead fish do—it turned belly up and floated towards the surface. Hoops decided to catch a ride to the top and breathe some fresh ocean air. He grabbed one of the tentacles and it pulled him up, up, up.

The humid air above the surface smelled like fish and sea life. The sky was a light purple color he'd seen before. The sun was directly overhead. *It can't be.* He spun around to view the sky behind him and saw the two crescent moons side by side nearing the horizon. Peeking around the beast, he saw the hazy outline of a distant island; a long yellow beach stretched for miles in each direction and a thick wall of green jungle.

Hoops had no interest in going back to that island, but he did find it interesting how the two worlds might be connected. They both bristled with natural beauty.

Both had a dominant predator that ruled the environment. Hoops was equally unlucky to have encountered them, but he was super proud of his discoveries: the ridgeback toxigator, and the cave-dwelling red cracken dobber.

Proud of his accomplishment, and equally exhausted from all the excitement of almost dying (again), Hoops set the time piece to six thirty, wound it, and gave the lid a very thorough rub. The electric particles made no distinction between air and water and swirled around him, both above and below the water's surface. He pushed himself away from the stinky carcass of the red cracken dobber so as not to bring it back home with him accidentally. Just then heard, an airy, raspy voice whispered his name,

"Worrrrrthingtooooooooon..." He spun around and was face to face with the skeletal remains of a dead mermaid floating on its side. Gray tangled hair hung in mossy streaks down the sides and back of her skull. Her eyes were there, but they were solid black orbs.

"I see you. I found you..." the voice hissed from behind the black eyes. Slowly, the mermaid's boney arm moved, reaching out for him.

Hoops was so freaked out he had stopped rubbing the timepiece without realizing it. "Leave me alone!" he yelled in anger.

"Bring it to me..." The skeleton wrapped its hand around the handle of a knife that was stuck between two of its ribs, the knife that someone had used to end its life ages ago. The blade scraped against bone as it slid from the ribcage, and the mermaid pulled itself close to Hoops. The eyes were alive, those inky black eyes.

Hoops rubbed the pocket watch with all his might. He was done with this nightmare. He was done with this world. He was done with exploring. He just wanted to get home.

Whoosh!

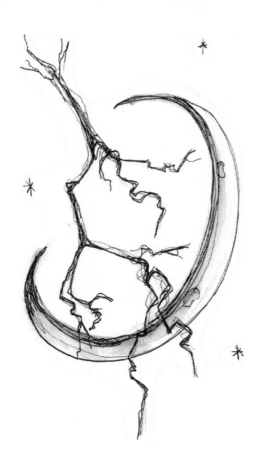

Sirihbaz

Soaking wet and exhausted, Hoops lay curled up in a ball, shivering violently. The cool fresh air around him smelled like dirt and pine. He lay on the ground, with rich green ferns all around him. He certainly wasn't in his bedroom. He checked the pocket watch and saw that it was set for five o'clock. He tried to make sense of what was happening. *I must have set it to five o'clock by mistake. Or maybe it reset itself again. It did that a few times on the very first day.*

Looking at the forest all around him, his eyes fell on delicate flowers and tall, thick, red-wooded trees. The little sunshine that made it through the canopy of leaves above was quite warm, but the air was devilishly cool. He knew that if he kept this wetsuit on for too long, he would catch a cold, or worse, get hypothermia. He walked over to one of these huge trees that had fallen long ago, broke some limbs off, gathered up some ferns and fallen branches, and made a little lean-to for shelter. Crawling inside, he took off the wetsuit and tried to dry himself off. As midday slid into afternoon, he found he wasn't getting much warmer, and his shaking was getting worse. Desperate for warmth, he found two dry sticks, and tried to start a fire by rubbing them together. But his hands were so cold and stiff, and his body was so chilly and shaky, he gave up in discouragement.

He threw the sticks away from him and started to cry. He was afraid, alone, and cold. He was done with exploration and only wanted to go home. As he sobbed with his head between his knees, he heard a squatty little voice in the ferns in front of him.

"Hush. Hush. Not too loud. Not too loud, now."

Hoops looked up to see a small, round manlike form waddling towards him from behind the fern. The little man couldn't have been more than three feet tall. Wiping the tears from his eyes, Hoops jumped up so quickly he banged his head on the fallen tree trunk.

"Ouch!"

"Easy, young traveler. I bear you no ill. No ill at all." It was a small dwarf wearing an animal-skin tunic and pants. He had a broad belt and a hat made of fern leaves. His nose was large and round, and his mouth and chin were buried deep within a brown scraggly beard with bits of leaves and grass throughout.

"There, there," the dwarf whispered as he slipped a pack off his fat roundish back. "Let me help you. On my word as a WolliPog, I am vowed to assist you. Yes, assist you." He pulled an animal-skin blanket out of the pack and tossed it around Hoops' shoulders. Immediately, Hoops felt soft warmth seeping back into his body.

"Thank you." He shivered. "How do you know I'm a traveler?"

"Hush. Hush. All your questions will be answered in time." The dwarf was nervous and looked around as he whispered, "Not now, though. Not now. Now is the time for being quiet and following old WolliTom."

Hoops decided to trust the kind dwarf and gathered his scuba gear and wetsuit laying on the ground.

"Leave that stinky mess, boy-o," the little man insisted. "It stinks of fish and pee. They'll be able to track us down with no magic but their noses." The dwarf looked at the timepiece on the ground, "You'd best hold on to that pretty thing, though. You don't want *him* gettin' hold of it. Or knowin' it's here again."

"Who are you talking about? Who's *him*?" Hoops asked, but WolliTom didn't answer. He was already scampering away, nervously checking the noises in the air and scanning the forest all around. He led the way through thick brush and around earthen mounds. He looked this way and that, always stopping suddenly when a bird would sing, or when the wind would blow. His fat little feet were bare but left no footprints. He moved in complete silence. Hoops, on the other hand, felt like a clumsy, loud goofball as he stomped behind the dwarf.

"Where are we going, WolliTom?"

"Green Dewin's place," the dwarf whispered. "He can help. Always helps the travelers."

They kept stalking through the forest until they came to an open field. On the other side was the tiny village of the WolliPogs. The roofs of their tiny homes were no more than six feet tall, and each one had a smoking little chimney, and little fences containing small gardens of flowers and vegetables. As they passed through the village, bearded fat faces smiled and waved. On the far side of the village, they came to a large red-wooded tree, just like all the others in the forest. WolliTom knocked on the trunk three times with his chubby little fist. A hidden door popped open right out of the wood, and a happy old voice inside said, "Come in, WolliTom! Did you bring him? Is he with you?"

"Yes, Dewin. Yes. He's here now." The dwarf led Hoops through the tree trunk and into a human-sized cabin! There was a great big fireplace with logs blazing, and comfy animal-skin couches in front of it. Standing next to the hearth was a tall, grey-bearded man in a forest-green cloak. He held a pot of freshly brewed tea.

"Pleased to meet you, young traveler. I am Green Dewin. I am the protector of the WolliPogs, keeper of the forest, and ally to all travelers. You would probably call me a wizard, but I don't like to brag about my magic." When he said *magic,* the smoke from the fireplace shot out into the room and formed the image of the timepiece.

Hoops almost forgot his manners. He had never seen real magic before. "I'm Worthington D. Hooper, but my friends call me…"

"Hoops!" the happy wizard interrupted. "Come and sit by my fire and get warm, boy. WolliTom, please fetch some new clothes for our guest."

The dwarf smiled and went his way back into the village to carry out Dewin's errand.

"Now tell me all about your journey through the Four Gates," the wizard said as he pulled out a writing quill and an old book.

"The four whats?" Hoops didn't have a clue what he meant.

"The first four worlds of the timepiece," the wizard explained. "They are the four trial worlds a traveler must pass through before they can explore the remaining five worlds. They are known as the Four Gates. Let's start with what you'd call 'one o'clock.'"

Hoops warmed himself and drank tea while giving Dewin every detail of his adventures on the island, in the mirror, the shadow world, and the underwater realm. He talked for hours while the wizard made notes in his book.

"You're a brave boy. And a true hero! It is indeed a pleasure to meet you and have you in my humble home. I'm sure you have some questions about some of the stranger things you've experienced, yes?"

Hoops nodded his head and said, "Two different times, I heard a voice. It whispered to me. It knew my name, and it came from a pair of black eyes. They looked like orbs made of ink. What *was* that?"

"That," Dewin explained, "was the voice of Braxo. He is the black wizard who terrorizes Sirihbaz."

"Sirihbaz?" Hoops had never thought that these worlds might have names. This was the first world where he met intelligent people who knew he was a traveler.

"You are in Sirihbaz now, Hoops. This is the world of wizards and enchantments. This is the world where magic lives. There is great beauty here, and wonders beyond what one can even begin to explain. But those who misuse the magic of this world, like Braxo, create misery, slavery, and darkness. Braxo seeks power above all and he knows that the timepiece exists, and that it is the only magic that will allow him to escape this world. If he gets the timepiece, he will take his dark magic to the other worlds to conquer them and enslave their peoples."

"But what about the eyes?" Hoops reminded the green wizard.

"Ah yes. Braxo cannot enter the other worlds yet, but he can look into them through the eyes of other creatures. When he casts his dark spells, the creature's eyes will turn black, and they won't know they are being used or controlled. He can speak to their minds, and manipulate their thoughts and feelings, and sometimes even control their bodies. It amazes me that he is now powerful enough to use even dead creatures, like that poor mermaid's skeleton."

Hoops shivered just thinking about that skull with the glowing black eyes. "How did he know my name?"

"I don't know. Braxo grows more powerful year by year. He knows that the travelers often make it through the Four Gates and into Sirihbaz. He's constantly seeking to trap any boy that arrives in Sirihbaz and steal the timepiece from him. You're in great danger, Hoops. In all the other worlds, he can see you, but here in Sirihbaz, he can capture you and hurt you. His magic is most powerful here."

"But I feel safe with you, here in your home." Hoops felt a real friendship between him and Dewin. Things began to make sense and he didn't want to leave, even though he knew he endangered himself and the WolliPog village.

"My forest magic is hopefully strong enough to hide you from his eyes, but once you leave my home, his eyes and ears will be everywhere. He probably knows you're here in Sirihbaz and he's already hunting for you, most likely."

"Can't you defeat him with *your* magic?"

"No. I can only protect the WolliPogs and keep the forest. I cannot do anything to strip Braxo of his power. I can only bring a bit of balance to this world. And if he were to travel to the other worlds, I'd have no way of stopping or slowing his destructive plans."

Hoops loved this beautiful world and its good creatures. The thought of leaving it behind with a black wizard growing more powerful made him feel awful.

"There has to be someone powerful enough to defeat him."

"Only the Oracle would know if that's true." Dewin smiled. "That is where you'll go next. The timepiece has already been set to seven o'clock and is ready for you to travel."

Hoops pulled out the pocket watch and saw that wise old Dewin was right. "What about the two moons I saw on the island?"

"When you were on the island of Isango and floating in its sea later, you saw the two worlds of Sirihbaz and Torpil. You're in one of those worlds now, the Oracle is on the other. And you will pass through more before..."

Thud, thud, thud. WolliTom banged on the door from outside. His knocking sounded frantic and panicked. As Dewin opened the door, the dwarf tossed a set of animal-skin clothes to him, then fell to the floor exhausted and bloodied. Through the door, Hoops saw that the entire village was on fire! WolliPogs ran everywhere, crying and screaming; some of them lay on the ground, not moving at all.

"He's here!" the wizard shouted at Hoops, "He's come for you. Quickly, Hoops! You must leave. NOW." Just then, a slender, black-cloaked wizard emerged from the village flames and walked towards Dewin's tree.

"Worthington!" that familiar voice hissed. "I've found you. Give it to me... NOW!" On the last word, he stretched out his long, skinny fingers and used his magic to throw Dewin against the wall and hold him there.

Hoops grabbed the bundle of clothing from the floor and rubbed the watch. The timepiece must not fall into Braxo's hands, but he felt like a coward for leaving his friends behind. Looking at Dewin as the electric particles swirled around him, he shouted, "I *will* come back. I *will* save Sirihbaz."

Braxo was furious. He pulled out a wicked knife with a blood-red, wavy blade and thrust it into Dewin's chest, then turned to face Hoops.

Whoosh!

Torpil

Hoops didn't care that he had traveled to a new world. He didn't open his eyes right away. He was crying. It hurt him deeply to watch his friend Green Dewin die. And poor WolliTom. His whole village had been destroyed.

It was all my fault. I should have left sooner. I spent too much time bragging about my adventures to the old wizard.

The tears kept coming. He cried until his eyes were red and dry, and his nose was snotty. "I'm so sorry," he whispered, getting up on his hands and knees. As his senses came back to him, he felt chilly and grabbed the bundle of clothes. Slipping on an animal skin tunic and pants, the warmth reminded him of WolliTom's kindness and he cried a little more. He strapped on a broad leather belt and noticed that on the right side, hung a beautiful dagger made of bluish steel, with a white-bone handle. On the left side of the belt was a pouch perfectly sized to hold the pocket watch. He also had a pair of snug little leather boots, and a fern-green hooded cape, with bits of grass and moss all over.

Looking around, he took in the beauty of Torpil. This was the first time he knew where he was, and why he was there. The thought of returning home, to the six thirty, made him feel like a quitter. He had to do something to help his new friends and going home just because he was afraid, would mean defeat. So, he set out to explore this new world and find this 'Oracle.'

He didn't have to walk very far to discover that he stood at the edge of a gorgeous canyon. All around him were thick glossy flowers of deep blues, purples, and pinks. The luminous petals sparkled, glowing in the darkness. It was night here. But the entire world was lit by a brilliant white full moon. Stars filled the sky with the most dazzling array of color. A sheet of blue light waved across a portion of the sky, making strange shapes. It reminded Hoops of the Aurora Borealis he'd seen in his geography books. With every wave of the blue light, the flowers and ground would sparkle and twinkle. Out of the corner of his eye, he caught a shimmer coming from a nearby tree, one of many in a lush grove of beautiful trees that ran all along the canyon edge in each direction. They were like maple trees, with pointed leaves, but they grew the strangest fruits he'd ever seen. Hoops shuffled over to the tree and grabbed a glassy globe-shaped fruit. It was made of crystal, and so heavy he almost dropped it! A tiny light danced inside of the crystal fruit and as Hoops placed both hands on it, the light within produced an image. He saw himself in the mirror world. He saw the burglars, and the gun. He watched himself grab the burglar's reflection by the wrist and save

Ms. Grankel. Then the crystal went dark. Dropping it to the ground, he grabbed another fruit off the tree and saw Smitty giving him the timepiece and the Traveler's Code. Each crystal had a memory of kindness or bravery. Someone had been watching his adventures and documenting the good things he had done or experienced. Many other crystals showed images of other boys who had saved friends, shown kindness to animals, or defeated villains.

Hoops was filled with hope. He knew there were powerful forces watching his good deeds and thought perhaps they could help him save his friends! He walked to the edge of the canyon and shouted, "Hello! Anyone there?"

A response echoed, *"WE'RE HERE. We're here, we're here..."*

He shouted again, "I'M WORTHINGTON!"

The echo replied, "HOOPER, Hooper, Hooper..."

He laughed aloud. "HA, HA."

"WHAT'S SO FUNNY? What's so funny, what's so funny?" the echo called back.

This was the most fun he'd had in a long time. Too bad his school buddies weren't there. They would love this! Then he thought about his new friends in

Sirihbaz and remembered he was on a mission.

"HOW DO I SAVE MY FRIENDS?" he shouted as loud as he could.

After several seconds of silence, the echo replied, "THE ORACLE KNOWS. The Oracle knows, the Oracle knows..."

"WHERE IS THE ORACLE?" he yelled back.

The canyon echoed, "BEHIND YOU. Behind you, behind you...."

Hoops spun around but saw no one. No people or creatures beyond the trees and flowers. But in the distance rose a conspicuous mountain. It was shaped like a tall and narrow cone, almost like a skinny volcano that shot up out of the ground and forgot to fatten. It was more of a rock tower that was broader at its base. Across the face of this mountain zigzagged a stone path carved into thousands of steps. And whatever was at the top of those steps couldn't be seen from the bottom.

He set off for the path and soon made it to the bottom of the mountain. Taking the first few steps, Hoops felt the ground beneath him tremble. It was faint, but he certainly didn't imagine it. It only lasted for about three seconds. He continued and about halfway up the mountain, it happened again. The ground shook and it was certainly more noticeable and lasted for about six seconds. Higher and higher he climbed. The zigzagging of the path became more frequent as the mountain became narrower. Almost to the top, the path stopped halfway across the narrow face of what was now a cliff. The stony path turned right and went straight through the rock and into a tiny cavern. The path continued off to the left through an opening at the other end of the cavern. Stalactites grew on the cavern ceiling, sparkling with purple gems reflecting the starlight coming from the opening at the other end. As Hoops stopped to take in this little cave's beauty, the ground shook. It was rough this time and lasted for about ten seconds. The rumblings grew worse, so he made the decision to climb to the top quickly.

Following the path on the other end took him on a very narrow walkway that wound itself around the tip top of the mountain. The top of the mountain was crater-like, about a hundred feet across and only six feet deep. The floor of the crater was bare as a desert except for the wishing well at the very center. Hoops knew this must be where he'd find the Oracle, so he ran to the well and yelled into it.

"HELLO!" His voice sounded cold and hollow as it echoed down the well. But the voice that came back was warm, calm, and welcoming.

"Hello, Traveler."

"Are you the Oracle?" Hoops knew it was a dumb question as soon as it came out of his mouth.

"Yes, of course. Are you Worthington?" replied the well.

"Yeah." Hoops thought about what to ask. "I've come to find out how to save my friends."

"Your friends will be saved," the Oracle reassured him. "But you must finish your travels first."

"Finish my travels? But I need to go back and save my friends first! What do I need to do to defeat Braxo?"

"You will not defeat Braxo. If you go back to Sirihbaz, you will be destroyed, and the timepiece will belong to the evil wizard. He will then use it to escape Sirihbaz and bring darkness to the other worlds. Only SHE can stop him."

"She?" Hoops was confused. "You mean a girl? What girl? I didn't see a girl in Sirihbaz."

"She is not in Sirihbaz. She is not yet a traveler. But she has been chosen to travel and will defeat Braxo."

"But I want to defeat him!" Hoops grew angry. These weren't the answers he had come for. "I want to kill him for what he did to my friends." Hoops pulled out his dagger and swung it back and forth through the air, stabbing an imaginary Braxo as he talked to the wishing well.

"You must finish your travels. Only then can the girl be found. Only then can your friends be saved." The Oracle wasn't changing its mind.

"But Dewin was killed right in front of me!" Hoops screamed at the Oracle. "He was my friend. He gave me answers." He kicked the well when he screamed the word 'answers.' Tears welled in his eyes.

"Ouch," the Oracle said calmly. "No need for that. I'm only telling you the truth as I have foreseen it. Your friend Green Dewin can be brought back, but only if you continue your travels."

"You mean Dewin will come back?!"

"You must go to Animas. Find a phoenix feather and bring it back to me. Then you must complete your travels. That is the only way you can help your friends and revive Dewin. That is the only way the girl can be found." The Oracle grew impatient.

"Animas? Is that the eight o'clock world?" Hoops asked as he pulled out his pocket watch and set it for eight o'clock.

"Yes," the Oracle whispered.

"How will I find the phoenix feather?" Hoops asked.

"You ask the wrong questions, boy!" The Oracle was getting angry. The ground shook so hard the rocks on the grounds jiggled. "Use the tools your friends have given you. The cloak, the knife, the watch." The ground cracked. "Finding the feather is easy. Getting the feather and returning here is your mission." The quaking worsened by the second. The entire world bounced in Hoops' eyes as it trembled and shook.

"Now GO!" screamed the angry Oracle as Hoops rubbed the timepiece.

Animas

Hoops was relieved that the ground wasn't shaking anymore. It was also nice to see some daylight again. He was in a forest of pine trees on the side of a big hill that stretched from a wild rushing river below up to a cliff face high above him.

A distant growly grumble came from a big brown bear down at the water's edge. Hoops recognized the shape of its head and the humped shoulder. It was a grizzly. The bear stood on its hind legs and looked up the hill towards Hoops. It was sniffing the air and caught the scent of the traveler. With a roar, the grizzly charged up the bank. Hoops had heard he was supposed to play dead if a bear ever attacked him, so he curled up in a ball, and covered himself completely with his mossy, grassy cloak that WolliTom had given him. The thud of the bear's paws and the snapping of twigs and pine needles grew louder and louder. But the bear charged right past him! It stopped a short distance past Hoops, stood, and sniffed the air again. Hoops could see through the fibers of the cloak quite easily and knew the bear must have lost sight of him. But bears could smell another animal more than a mile away, so Hoops just lay completely still. He held his breath, too. He wouldn't make a move or a sound.

The irritable bear turned towards him and stopped only inches away. Hoops could see the vicious, enormous, black claws, and the bear's giant nose sniffing the ground surrounding the cloak. But the bear didn't attack Hoops. After a few minutes of snorting and sniffing, the grumpy bear moaned and plodded back down to the water's edge.

Hoops was completely invisible to the bear under the cloak, and the bear hadn't been able to see or smell him. "Whew!" He let out a heavy sigh, grateful that WolliTom had given him such a fine gift. He stood slowly and silently so as not to alarm the bear. He donned the cloak and made sure that he covered his head with the hood. While he walked, birds would swoosh by his head chirping and calling, and the squirrels (nature's most nervous critter) would continue digging for fallen nuts in the soft dirt without a clue or care that a big human boy was about to step on them. It became obvious to Hoops that while he wore the cloak's hood, the animals of the forest could neither see nor hear him.

Just for fun, he stepped in front of a bobcat crouched just outside a rabbit's hole. It prepared to pounce as soon as the unlucky bunny had the bad sense to emerge from the hovel. Hoops estimated the distance between his toes and the crouched predator was only about three feet. He raised his hands up to his head, grabbed the hood of his cloak, and flicked it back. The bobcat's whole body jolted as if it had just brushed an electric fence, and it jumped straight up in the air in surprise. Its feet dangled in the air and trailed behind it as it lifted off. It must have flown ten feet straight up like a cheap firework, then came back down in the same spot. When it hit the ground, it made quite an ungraceful scramble to get on its feet and ran off into the woods. Hoops' side ached from laughing so hard.

Off to find the phoenix, Hoops took inventory of what little he knew of the mythical bird.

"One," he told himself aloud as he extended his forefinger. "The bird can live for hundreds of years. Two"—he extended his second finger—"The bird creates a nest before it dies and when it's time, it bursts into flames." Extending a third finger, he continued, "Three, a new phoenix is born from the pile of the dead phoenix's ashes." He guessed that if he needed a phoenix feather, he had to find the nest, and either snatch a feather from the bird just before it burned, or pluck a feather from the young bird as soon as it was born. "Either way," he continued aloud, "I have to find the nest. My guess is that it will be someplace high and out of reach of any predators." He turned towards the cliff face that begun at the top of the slope on his left.

The cliff shot straight up a hundred feet then plateaued into a flat mountaintop. "I bet I can get a good look at the whole area from up there!" Slipping the hood back over his head, he scrambled up the hill and reached the foot of the cliff. He hadn't really climbed much as a kid, other than the occasional playground equipment and a plastic climbing wall inside a sporting goods store. He knew it was important not to look down and remembered someone telling him he needed complete focus on just finding the next foothold or handhold. Step by step, he found his way, slowly crawling up the face of the cliff. He never tried to guess if he was halfway up, or how far down the ground might be. He didn't think of anything except where he'd place his hand or foot next. His mind burned with focus, and he felt a strange sense of peace and freedom as he tackled his climb.

At last, he reached the top. As Hoops pulled his shoulders up over the edge, he needed to grab a rock, or vine, or root. That would help him pull the rest of his body up and he could finally rest. But there was nothing but sand and pebbles at the cliff's edge. The muscles in his arms and legs burned from exhaustion. He knew he didn't have a lot of energy left and if he didn't figure something out quickly, he would panic. He slipped his hand down to his new dagger and drew it out. He raised his arm and plunged the dagger into the dirt in front of him. He imagined the blue steel stabbing into Braxo's heart, which just made him stab harder. With the knife deeply in the ground, it made the perfect anchor and Hoops used his remaining strength to pull his entire body off the cliff wall and onto the flat dirt.

All he could do was roll over onto his back and breathe. Relief flooded his limbs, and as the cool dry wind and the warm sun cast their spell on him he fell asleep.

His dreams were very strange. He slid along the ground on his belly. He could feel the sand and rocks scraping by, and he could slip through the tiniest spaces between rocks and shrubs. He was a snake. His long, powerful body would twist and squeeze and wind its way forward with ease. He flicked his tongue out and a rush of sensation filled his mouth. He felt the heat of a very large animal near him. He couldn't see the world around him that well, but he could feel its heat and that was just as good. He slithered towards the animal and slid over its leather boots. The creature lay flat on the ground. Sliding up the leg, he coiled himself on the large creature's chest. It was soft and warm, covered with an animal-skin shirt. The creature had one arm extended with its hand holding a bone-handled blue knife. It was Hoops' sleeping body! He decided to get a different point of view and slid off the chest, winded his way to a nearby rock, and coiled himself up, facing the boy's sleeping body. As he took in the sight and heat through his snaky tongue, he realized this wasn't a dream at all. This was Animas! He was inside the snake's mind.

His sleeping boy body turned his head, then rolled over to get more comfortable. As it did, the dagger slipped out of his hand. Everything went black! Hoops was jolted awake. And he sat straight up. He lifted his hands and looked at them and felt himself all over. He was back in his own body, sitting up with his legs stretched straight out in front of him.

He felt an icy fear on the back of his neck and turned his head to the left. There on a rock only five or so feet from him was the biggest rattlesnake he'd ever seen! Its diamond pattern was dark and beautiful, running the length of its entire body. The snake rattled, not appreciating having its mind hijacked.

Hoops knew he was moments away from being bit, and that would mean certain death for a boy alone in the wilderness! His only defense was to pick up the knife and back away slowly. He slowly slid his hand forward along the ground and over the handle. When he picked up the blade, it vibrated in his hand. He pointed it at the snake and closed his eyes. A tingle in his stomach signaled something had changed, and when he opened his eyes again, he looked at his own boy body standing upright with the knife pointed at him. He was in control of the snake again, inside its mind and body! *This is powerful magic!*

WHAM!

He was knocked off his rocky perch by something. Dazed from the impact, he couldn't make sense of what just happened until he looked around for his boy body. It was down below him getting smaller and smaller. He felt cold, black talons squeezing him, and when he flicked his tongue out, it was filled with the feathery scents and heat of a large bird. It was an eagle, carrying him high up over the pine forest, the river, and all the rest of it. They rose high above the plateau and skimmed just above a cloud. Hoops saw in the distance, a volcano poking its cratered head through thick clouds miles and miles away. *The phoenix must be there.* But this eagle wasn't going to the volcano. It was headed to its nest for dinner, and as soon as this eagle got Hoops to its nest, it would devour him. But he wouldn't be eaten without a fight. In fact, as a rattlesnake, he had some special tools he would love to share with this screechy bird.

He locked his eyes on the eagle's leg just above where the claw meets the thigh, flexed his muscles, and struck as hard as he could. He could feel his fangs easily slip into the eagle's meaty leg, past feathers, and all the way down to the bone. Once he had sunk his fangs into the eagle, he pumped venom through them. It was only a matter of time.

The eagle weakened and became woozy, opening its talons to release the snake, but Hoops didn't let go. He held onto the bird with his fangs and dangled like the string of a kite. They descended lower and lower and eventually, they were just over the plateau. The eagle's heart finally stopped mid-air and it dropped straight down to the ground, landing in a 'poof' of dust and feathers. Hoops landed on top of the bird and survived the fall with no harm done.

He closed his eyes and summoned the feeling in his stomach again. Back in his own boy body, he lowered the knife and went over to look at the fallen eagle. What a beautiful creature it was. A majestic golden eagle. He remembered reading about this species. It was the most skilled winged hunter in the sky. He felt terrible for having killed this bird. But when he was in the snake's body, all he cared about was survival, and his instinct was to strike. Now, in his own body, he felt sadness and regret. Careful not to get too close to the snake, he gathered rocks and placed them all around and on top of the dead eagle, marking a grave for the fallen raptor.

The snake slithered its way to the top of the rocky pile and disrespectfully coiled itself up and rattled at Hoops.

"Get off!" he screamed, but the snake just rattled, taunting him.

"I hate you!" he continued "I wish you had fallen to your death!" Hoops slipped his dagger out and stepped towards the rattlesnake. The rattle grew louder and louder, warning the boy to keep away.

That rattle was a warning to Hoops, but also served as a dinner bell for more hungry eagles. WHAM! Another golden eagle slammed into the snake from above. The snake twisted and struck, but the eagle had a claw just below its head, keeping the snake's fangs out of reach. Hoops watched as the eagle held the snake against the rocky dirt while it poked and ripped with its beak. Eventually, the snake stopped moving, dead. Free from danger, the eagle lifted into the air with its dinner dangling in its talons. This was a perfect opportunity and Hoops wasted no time. Pointing the knife at the great bird, he sensed the vibration of the blade in his hand. When he closed his eyes, he felt the tingle in his stomach again.

The Feather

Hoops remembered seeing the world from an airplane window once. The cars looked like little ants and the colors and shapes of cities and farms stretched on and on forever. But seeing the world through an eagle's eyes was far more exciting. He could see a small groundhog poke his head out of a hole from miles away. He could see fish jumping in the river and could almost count their scales as he soared high above in the clouds. The best part was the feeling of the cold air on his eyeballs and the sound of the wind as it slipped over his gliding form.

As he pumped his wings a few times, he noticed the weight of the snake in his claws. He didn't really care to have dinner right now, so he pumped higher and higher until he was at cloud altitude. Hovering for a moment, he let go of the snake's body and enjoyed watching its long fall. It splattered on the rocks below and Hoops felt like the world was a tiny bit better with one less rattlesnake.

He glided and soared for a little while, getting used to the freedom of flight and enjoying the tickle and rush he felt inside as he would dive and loop and twist through the air. Climbing above a nearby cloud, he flew in a wide circle scanning the horizon until he saw the volcano's peak in the distance. *There.* With the wind at his back, he pumped and soared towards the mountain of fire.

This was an active volcano. Deep in its crater, a pool of lava swirled, bubbling and churning. The heat from it made it difficult to fly downward into the crater so Hoops glided along the edge, searching the inside wall for any signs of the phoenix. About halfway between the lava and the top of the volcano, about fifty feet or so, was a small, flat stone slab sticking out from the face of a rocky wall. On the slab was a tangle of freshly fallen green limbs and long grass twisted into a very tidy nest. Also weaved into the nest with the limbs and grass, were bright red feathers! *If I can just pluck one of those feathers out of the nest, I'm home free!* He dove into the crater and flew alongside the wall to avoid as much heat as possible. Reaching the nest, he landed carefully and tugged at the limbs and feathers. The nest was built so perfectly that Hoops had trouble getting a feather free. Still, he kept working at it. The heat from the volcano was unbearable. His eyes burned like when he would get soap or shampoo in them. He could barely open them, and he could feel his skin under his feathers sweating and stinging from the hot air.

SCREEECH!

An enormous bright red bird thundered from above. Hoops knew he had trespassed into the home of the phoenix and now he'd been caught. The huge red bird dove into the volcano towards the nest with its talons reaching forward to strike and kill. It was time to fly! Hoops jumped out of the nest just as the phoenix plunged into it. Hoops pumped and pumped, not looking behind him at all. He used the hot air of the volcano to lift him out of the mountain. The phoenix had hit the nest so hard, it was briefly tangled in the limbs. This gave Hoops just enough time to get out of the crater and put some distance between him and the red terror behind him. As he reached the top, he dove over the edge and into the cloud below to pick up more speed.

SCREECH!

The phoenix was furious and chased him through the cloud. The fiery red wings beat the air and Hoops could hear the thud, thud, thud behind him. He glanced back and saw that the phoenix was gaining on him. He dove again to gain speed. As he did, he saw the small plateau in the distance. His great eyesight caught the form of his boy body standing near a pile of stones with his knife still pointing up into the air. *If I can get the phoenix close enough and time it just right...*

He pumped and dove, pumped and dove. The enraged phoenix was right behind him, but Hoops kept a few yards of air between them. When he was finally directly overhead of his boy body, he tucked his wings in and dove straight down. He closed his eyes and summoned the tingle in his stomach again.

Hoops flung his eyelids open and looked straight up. The eagle was still high up in the sky but quickly approached. His shoulder felt like it was on fire, having held the knife up for so long. But he had just enough strength left to raise the blue blade directly over his head. When the eagle realized he was diving towards a human, it spread out its wings and whirled to the side. Hoops felt the wind from the bird on his face but kept looking skyward. The red phoenix was just behind the eagle and didn't notice the boy until the eagle flew out of the way. Hoops pointed the knife at the fiery bird and waited to feel the vibration. The blade buzzed in his hand, signaling that the moment had come. He closed his eyes and felt the flutter inside.

Hoops spread his monstrous crimson wings out and pumped as hard as he could. Barely missing his boy body, he swooped to the side and hovered for a few seconds, then dropped to the ground. The dirt felt like ice on his claws and talons as if he had just plunged them into a snowy river. He hopped and turned to face the boy body holding the knife straight up over his head. *I can't believe it worked! I am the phoenix.*

The thought of being in the mind and body of a legendary creature scared him. He had already killed a majestic golden eagle, destroyed a diamondback rattlesnake, and had nearly caused another eagle to be killed. He had no interest in endangering the beautiful phoenix, too. He arched his neck backwards and used his beak to pluck the longest tail feather he could feel right out of his butt. SCREECH! It stung when he pulled it out, making his backside itch like crazy. With the feather in his beak, he hopped and waddled over to the boy body and tucked the feather under his belt. Then with a great pump of his wings, he leapt into the sky and took off towards the volcano. When he had risen above the clouds, he whispered, "Thank you, my friend," then closed his eyes and returned to his own boy body.

When Hoops dropped his arm, the knife fell to the ground. He was exhausted and couldn't move his arm at all. It was completely numb and cold, and he had no sensation for several minutes. Then it itched, burned, and ached as the blood returned. When the agony was over, he slipped the feather from his belt and examined it. It was warm in his hand and smelled stinky, like a firework that had just gone off. It was about two feet long and fiery red. It was almond shaped and about five inches wide in the middle. It was the most beautiful feather he'd ever seen. But what he loved most about it was that it would somehow help him save Green Dewin.

Taking one last look around at Animas, he drew a deep full breath of clean, cool air. He opened the pouch on the left side of his belt and pulled out the timepiece. He set the hands to seven o'clock, wound the timepiece, and rubbed its lid. With the magic of the pocket watch swirling around him, he said goodbye to the rocky grave of the eagle and to the wild natural beauty of the kingdom of animals.

Whoosh!

Hoops opened his eyes to the sparkling moonlit night sky of Torpil. He lay flat on his back, within a stone's throw of the wishing well. All was calm with no signs of quakes; no cracked or split ground, or disturbed rocks. He stood and respectfully walked to the Oracle. A warm and welcoming voice bubbled up from its dark well.

"You've returned, Traveler. Well done."

"Yeah. I'm back and I brought your stupid feather, too." He didn't think it was a stupid feather at all. He thought it was gorgeous, but he didn't like that the Oracle had told him someone else would defeat Braxo.

"Well done, indeed. Give me the stupid feather, young one." The Oracle was sarcastic sometimes. It reminded him of his mom.

Hoops pulled the feather from his belt and admired the deep hues of red and its almond shape. He wouldn't miss its smell. Holding it over the well, he said in a loud voice, "For Green Dewin," then dropped the feather into the well. He watched as it twirled downward, rocking back and forth, and slipping into the darkness below. A few moments later, a flash of light, charged by glowing dust particles, swirled out of the well into the sky above. Hoops had to cover his eyes from the brightness. It was a column of magic light. It bent and danced for just a few seconds, then slid back into the well and vanished.

"Green Dewin lives. Your friend will recover," the Oracle reassured him.

Hoops felt so relieved and grateful, he took a deep breath and sighed. "Thank you."

The Oracle wasted no time, "Your time here is now at an end. You must complete your travels." The ground trembled and shook, a gentle quake warning Hoops that it was time to go.

He popped open the timepiece, set it for nine o'clock, and gave it the gentle rub with his thumb. The dust in the air illuminated and traced its circles around him once again. He closed his eyes and held his breath.

Hapis

Rain. Cold, drizzling rain quickly soaked Hoops, like a winter storm that somehow made his insides feel wet and chilly. His animal skin shirt didn't help that much. He pulled the hood of his cloak over his head and wrapped himself as best as he could while he tried to find something to stand under. The sky was a blanket of grey clouds that made everything else look the same—grey, cold, sad, and dark. He was in the square of a village or town. All the buildings were identical, made of stone blocks with dark wood trim and beams. The roof of every house was either thatched with straw or shingled with tree bark. Also, every house had a chimney, but not one was smoking. There didn't seem to be any warmth in this place. Beyond the shingled rooftops on the other side of the square, Hoops could see a distant stone tower. The enormous structure dominated everything around it. But it was also simple in its design, a stone cylinder with parapets and ramparts atop. Lights shined from some of its tiny stone windows.

Hoops had no interest in this world and looked forward to moving on. He pulled out the pocket watch and set it for ten o'clock, but the hands slid back to nine o'clock on their own.

"Dang it," Hoops mumbled. "I guess I'll just have to do my time here." Wet and miserable, he walked through the town, looking for his next adventure. Every street was the same, filled with mud and cobblestone, and boring, sad, stone houses on both sides. Occasionally, he'd see someone walking on the other side of the street, but he kept his hood on and remained invisible. The people who lived here were fat and flabby, with oversized blobby noses hanging down over their frowning, grumpy faces. Every single citizen of this drab village looked the same, except for the shade of grey tunic each decided to wear that day, or hair which was either shaved entirely or tied back in a black, matted ponytail. This was the only way to tell if the person was a male or a female. He had no interest in talking to anyone who lived in this depressing place. He just wanted to find some place warm and dry. Looking at his feet, Hoops rounded the next corner. He didn't notice the dumpy, grumpy fellow coming around the same corner until he ran right into him. When Hoops bounced backwards off the person's fat, flabby tummy, his hood slipped off his head.

"Watch where you're going, you little toad turd!" the grump bellowed. When he talked, Hoops only noticed a few big, rotten teeth, and the fat of his neck jiggled almost as much as his round blobby nose. "Little rodents like you should be locked up just for breathing my air on this beautiful day."

Beautiful day? This guy is an idiot. He then remembered his manners and said, "I'm terribly sorry, sir. Please excuse me." He stepped aside and continued on his way.

Behind, him he heard grumpy pants shout, "EXCUSE ME?! Did you say 'Excuse me? How DARE you talk to me like that, you little bucket of roach vomit! I'll have you arrested, you hear me?"

Hoops was frightened. He didn't know what he'd done wrong. Trying to make peace, he said, "It was an accident, sir. I'm really sorry."

"SIR?! I'm a woman, you blind little maggot!"

Hoops hadn't noticed the ponytail. *Oops.*

"Call the guardsman!" she yelled across the street. Another grumpy-faced villager hurried off around a corner with a flabby nod of his shaved head. The woman grabbed Hoops by the arm, "You'll learn some respect soon enough."

A moment later, the guardsman appeared. He looked the same except he wore a cone-shaped helmet with a piece of metal hanging down to protect his onion-sized nose. He also carried a spear. The woman explained that Hoops had said, "Excuse me, please," and had then called her a "sir." The guardsman grunted and grabbed Hoops, tied his hands behind his back, and marched him away.

"Please, sir," Hoops begged the guardsman as they walked. "I don't know what I did wrong!"

"Keep your mouth SHUT, you little maggot," the guardsman snapped, "or I'll shut it for ya."

He led Hoops to a main street running directly to the foot of the huge stone tower. They crossed an open drawbridge with two guardsmen on each side. They spit on the ground and grimaced at him as he passed. Hoops was led into a round chamber that was empty except for a wooden desk raised several feet by a stone platform, and sitting behind it was an older, uglier, frumpy grump. He wore a white curly wig and a black robe. On the wall behind the desk, just above the grumpy judge's head was a wooden sign that read,

"NO GOOD DEED SHALL GO UNPUNISHED"

The guardsman explained to the judge what had happened, that Hoops had said "Excuse me, please," and "Sir."

The judge's frown got deeper and deeper as he listened, and his fat hairy eyebrows raised up before he shouted, "MANNERS? Here in Hapis? This will not do!" He grabbed his gavel and pointed it at Hoops. "Young man, you have violated the law. You have been charged with committing manners in a public place. The sentence is life in prison!" The gavel came down and banged his desk. "Take this maggot away and lock him up with the rest of them!" he barked at the guardsman.

They escorted Hoops into a small room and took everything away from him: his animal-skin shirt, pants, boots, his cloak, the belt and dagger, and the pouch that had the timepiece tucked inside. Luckily, they didn't bother to look in the pouch. They tossed a wadded-up bundle of clothes at him and ordered him, "Put this on, you little toad." Hoops unrolled the clothes and slipped on the shirt and pants. They were covered top to bottom in vertical black stripes. Between each black stripe was a different color of the rainbow. It was the first color Hoops had seen since arriving in the gloomy world, and he loved his new clothes. They were as soft as a fleece blanket, and so warm he didn't even need socks or shoes. He almost said 'thank you' to the guardsman but realized that it wouldn't end well for him if he did. The guardsman grabbed him by the arm and took him down a long set of stone steps that circled along the tower wall. When they got to his cell, the guardsman pushed Hoops inside and slammed the bars shut. He grunted at Hoops, then waddled back up the stairs.

Hoops panicked. He had never been separated from the timepiece before. His only hope was that the grumpy guardsmen didn't look through his things. Thinking about home, and his mom, and King Tut, he sat on his bed (which was super bouncy and comfy) and cried. The words of the Traveler's Code floated through his mind, and he sang to himself,

"It's not an adventure
'til something goes wrong.
You can only be brave when you're scared.
Through Four Gates and Five Worlds
by watch or by song,
Your journey is meant to be shared.

Adventures are wasted
on those who don't learn.
Adventures must come to their ends.
But there's always another one
'round the next curve.
And in Traveler's Rest, you'll find friends.

So, cheer up, young traveler,
Adventure awaits!
The timepiece has chosen you to roam.
And no matter the time
or where you go next,
At six thirty, you'll always come home.."

"That's a beautiful song," a voice called from the hallway. It was a woman's voice.

"Who's there?" Hoops whispered.

"I'm Myra."

He jumped up and leaned his head against the bars, looking down the hallway. All the other cells were along the wall like his and faced the same direction. They were arranged in such a way that the inmates couldn't see each other.

"How do I get out of here?"

"Shhh! Not so loud," Myra warned, "or the Frumps will hear you."

Hoops whispered this time, "How do I get out of this place?"

"Well, if I knew that, I wouldn't still be in here, would I?" Myra giggled. "Let's talk tomorrow at lunch. I'll introduce you to everyone. Get some sleep, Traveler."

"How do you know I'm a traveler? Myra. *Myra!* How do you know I'm a traveler?" His whispers were answered with silence. He curled up on his bed and slipped his blanket over his shoulders. It was like lying on a warm fleece cloud. Sleep came instantly and brought no dreams. When he awoke, his body was refreshed and his mind clear. He took note of everything he'd seen and heard in hopes that he could formulate a plan to retrieve the timepiece.

After about an hour of quiet concentrated planning, Hoops heard the heavy plod, plod, plod of footsteps, and the jingle of keys. The guardsman unlocked his cell and grunted, "Out." Hoops obeyed as the guardsman grabbed him by the arm and escorted him to the dining chamber, which was a big rectangular room on the floor below the cells. Ten rows of long wooden tables stretched from the back all the way up to the entrance, where a line of rainbow-striped people stood quietly in line. They waited to receive their bowl of grub, whispering to each other as they watched the guardsman lead the new kid to the back of the line.

"Don't make trouble! Or noise." The guardsman let go and shuffled out of the room. *Strange. The guardsmen leave the room and don't monitor the inmates as they talk and eat.*

When his turn came, and he was finally at the front of the line, he took a wooden bowl from atop a big stack and held it out in front of him. The frumpy grump serving the grub had a ponytail covered with a fishnet and wore an apron that was once white. She filled her ladle with a lumpy-looking soup and plopped it into his bowl. "Next!" she barked.

Hoops looked over the rows of tables for a spot to sit by himself. He didn't want to take someone else's favorite spot and make trouble with any of the other prisoners. Though, he didn't think it was likely any mean people were actually kept prisoner here. Everyone seemed quite normal and polite. People smiled at each other and whispered, "Good morning," and "Hello," and "Excuse me." Hoops even heard one prisoner say, "Thank you, buddy," to another. *This place is bizarre.*

Out of the corner of his eye, someone waved. It was a redheaded woman looking directly at him. When he turned his head towards her, she motioned for him to sit next to her. As he set the bowl on the table and sat down, she said quietly, "You did well not to say 'thank you' to the cook. She would have thrown her ladle at you."

"Are you Myra?" Hoops asked the redhead. She was a beautiful woman about his mom's age, maybe a little younger. And her smile was friendly and warm.

"That's right. I'm in the cell next to yours. And you are..."

"Hoops." He smiled. "Pleased to meet you." As they talked, another three inmates sat in front of them across the table, three grown men with smiles, manners, and an interest in meeting the new kid and hearing his story.

"These are my friends, Hoops. This is Doc," Myra said, pointing to an older bald man with glasses. He didn't have any facial hair and the wrinkles around his face told Hoops he was wise and kind. "This is Jonathan," she continued. Jonathan was a younger, muscular man with a thick black beard, a scar on his forehead, and a playful mischief in his eyes. "And this is Chase," she finished. Chase was a thin, tall, teenager with straight, jet-black hair, brown eyes, and thick black glasses.

"My name is Steven, but it took the Frumps a week to catch me, so Chase is my nickname. It was quite a week. Never ran so much in my life. Their fat legs don't let them run very fast." Chase seemed like a cool, older kid.

"Tell us about your travels, son." Doc leaned close and slurped his soup.

"How did you know I'm a traveler?"

"Are you gonna eat that?" Jonathan interrupted. "It's not as good once it's cold."

Hoops took a sip of his soup and found that it was delicious! It was like a homemade stew of beef, vegetables, and sweet spices. He was so confused. Prison food was supposed to be gross. Prison beds were supposed to be hard. Prison clothes were supposed to be itchy. And prisoners were supposed to be mean and dangerous. *Everything is backwards here. I almost* like *being in prison.*

Myra spoke, "You're not the first traveler we've met, Hoops. We get them in here all the time. I think it's part of their journey. We help them escape, and they all say the same thing, 'I'll come back and set you free,' but they never do. They never come back. But a new one always comes along and makes the same promise."

Hoops remembered saying the same thing to Dewin when he left Sirihbaz. The look of sad memories was obvious to the other inmates.

"It's okay, kid," Jonathan reassured him. "We love to help the travelers. Whether they come back or not, it gives us something fun to do..."

"...and the it drives the Frumps crazy when they can't figure out how someone escaped!" Chase obviously loved to play tricks on the Frumps. "Watch this!" He jumped up with his empty bowl and walked to the front of the line. "How about another bowl of that pig vomit you call food, you hag!" he shouted at the cook. She smiled at the insult and scooped another giant ladle of stew and plopped it in his bowl. Returning to his seat, he said, "You gotta know how to talk to the Frumps to get what you want. You have to have the opposite of manners."

Hoops was impressed. "Can you guys help me get my stuff back?" He hoped they would help one more traveler make his escape.

"Of course!" Doc smiled. "Your stuff is locked up in the warden's office. We just need to sneak you in there. Then we can get you to the tunnel."

Hoops felt alive with hope. "There's a *tunnel?*"

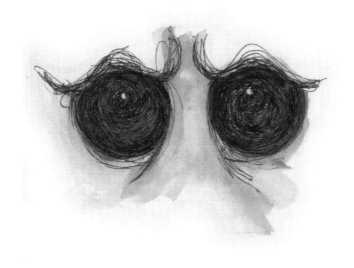

Escape

Breakfast the next morning was oatmeal filled with raisins and drizzled with maple syrup. Hoops shoveled in a mouthful as he fired question after question at Myra and the three men.

"I was thinking about this all night and I don't understand. If you guys have a tunnel, and you've helped travelers escape in the past, why don't you just leave? You could get out any time you wanted. Why do you stick around?"

Myra was surprised at the question. Hoops was smarter than many of the travelers that had come through the prison before him. Before she answered him, she looked at Doc, Jonathan, and Chase; each one nodded an approval in a silent vote.

"We're not prisoners at all, Hoops. We're spies."

Hoops' eyes widened and a dribble of delicious oatmeal fell from the side of his mouth onto the table.

"What? No way!"

"SHHHH!" Doc warned, "Let's keep it down, shall we? Whispers only. Please, Hoops."

"Sorry," Hoops hushed. "Who are you spying on? No, wait. Dumb question. Who are you spying *for*?"

Myra leaned in close after looking around to ensure they wouldn't be overheard.

"We serve Queen Diambi. She's been leading the resistance against the Marsh

Trolls for several years. We report on their military movements and numbers."

"Marsh Trolls?" Hoops asked.

"The Frumps, genius." Chase smirked.

Myra continued, "We've been at war for a long time. And they've grown stronger and more numerous over the past couple of years. But the resistance is growing as well, and eventually, we'll put Diambi back on her throne."

"Long live the queen," Jonathan whispered.

"Long live the queen." echoed Doc, Myra, and Chase.

After a short pause, so as not to be disrespectful, Hoops asked, "Myra, how often do you report to your queen? Don't the guardsmen notice when you're gone?"

Myra smiled, "We don't leave. We stay put and keep our eyes and ears open. We listen to the warden and the judge, and the guardsmen. They gossip, and complain, and moan about everything their leaders tell them to do. And when a traveler comes through the prison, we ask him to deliver the updates to the queen once we've helped them escape."

"Like an agreement!" Hoops interrupted. "You help me escape, and in exchange, I deliver your report to your queen before continuing my travels."

"Exactly."

"You've got a deal, Myra." Hoops took the last spoonful of oatmeal. "So what's the plan?"

"Chase and Jonathan will create a distraction here in the dining hall. When the warden leaves his office, you, Doc, and I will slip out of our cells and grab your belongings. Then we'll all meet back at the tunnel. I'll give you the message to deliver to the queen, and the directions to find her, just before you go into the sewer."

"The sewer?!" Hoops didn't like the sound of wading through Frumpy poop at all.

"You want to continue your travels, don't you?"

"Yeah. Of course. I just... you know... it's poop." Hoops imagined what the smell would be like and lost his appetite. "Yuck."

Myra continued, "Chase and Jonathan, you'll have to make sure you create enough noise to attract all the guardsmen AND get the warden to come out of her room. Then you can slip out through the rat shaft."

Hoops asked what the rat shaft was, and Jonathan pointed to the ceiling. Just behind one of the beams in the corner was a hole the size of a beach ball tucked away in the shadows.

"It's been there for years and they've never even noticed." Jonathan smirked.

"And if they catch us before we climb into the rathole, they'll just put us in the hole for a week. No big deal."

Chase jumped in, "But if they catch you leaving the prison, Hoops, you'll be executed."

"It'll be tonight. At lights out," Myra ordered. "Long live the queen."

"Long live the queen," they replied. Hoops echoed them.

****

Hoops sat on his bed going over the plan. His stomach felt like it was turning flips. He was ready to just get this escape over with. He bounced his legs up and down and tossed and turned in his bed. The waiting was torture! Hours passed, and Hoops occupied himself by making a list of all the creatures he'd discovered and all the friends he'd made. He still felt like a fool for not traveling with a journal. He was determined to write it all down when he got home.

"PSSST!"

Hoops looked out into the hall through the cell bars. Jonathan and Chase tiptoed up to his cell, "We'll meet you, Myra, and Doc at the tunnel." Chase pulled a key-shaped bone out of his pocket and picked the lock to Hoops' cell. "It's unlocked, but keep it closed and don't come out of your cell until AFTER the warden passes by."

"Good luck, Chase," Myra whispered from the next cell over. "Stay close to Jonathan and be careful."

Jonathan and Chase snuck down the hallway, moving from shadow to shadow. The plan was to lock themselves in the dining hall and make noise. Chase would use his key to lock the door, then join Jonathan in making the noise. Eventually, the warden would have to bring the keys to unlock the dining hall. That should give them plenty of time to escape through the rat shaft. When they got there, Jonathan went straight into the kitchen area and knocked things over. He threw big pots against the stone walls, shattering them to bits. He grabbed metal ladles and began banging on the iron cauldrons. He even began shouting, "Where's my food, you big toad munchers!" and "Marsh Trolls smell like rotten cabbage left in a used diaper!" He yelled as loud as he could and banged the pots and pans as hard as he could. He needed to make more noise.

"Chase, get over here and give me a hand, would you? Chase?" He turned towards the door and saw that it was still wide open... and Chase was *gone.* "Chase!" he shouted. But Chase didn't answer. Instead, two guardsmen hurried into the room. Jonathan ran to the other end of the room to get to the rat shaft, but a guardsman got there first. He was trapped. Chase had betrayed him and disappeared. One guardsman grabbed Jonathan with his fat, meaty hand, but Jonathan was stronger than most men. With a swing of his arm, he smashed his fist into the blobby-onion sized nose and the guardsman was knocked out cold. Three more Frumps charged into the room. Jonathan ran to the very back and jumped up on the end of one of the long tables. The guardsmen were forced to climb up on the table one at a time, making a line down the table. And one by one, they were knocked out by Jonathan's fists. He was a warrior and had fought thousands of Frumps on the battlefield. The room filled with Frumps when finally, one of them shouted, "Get the warden!"

****

Hoops saw guardsmen rush by his cell. Dozens of Frumps headed to the dining hall. All of a sudden, a huge marsh troll, dressed in black from head to toe, walked by. Gold circle earrings hung in each ear, and a silver ponytail hung down to its knees. It was two feet taller than all the others, and had a face covered in scars. As the warden marched past, Hoops

- 143 -

saw a grey-steeled sword with a jagged curved blade in its hand.

Myra and Doc slipped out of their cells and checked around the corner. "All clear, Hoops. Let's go!"

Hoops pushed the bars open and followed them down the dark, empty hallway and into the warden's office. There was nothing but a small wooden cot against the wall, a nasty-smelling toilet in the corner, and a huge desk. Behind the desk was a pile of junk on the floor. The warden had been collecting all the confiscated items from new prisoners for a long time. On the top of the pile was an animal-skin tunic, pants, leather boots, and the cloak. Hoops slipped them on and pulled his belt from the junk heap as well. The dagger still hung from it, and the pouch had remained unopened. The timepiece was still tucked neatly inside. *Whew.*

****

Back in the dining hall, a pile of guardsmen covered the floor around the table. Jonathan was still battling one Frump at a time, landing his fists with precision. But he was getting tired. A loud roar broke into the room, "STOP! He's mine." The warden strode to the table and jumped up quite quickly. The warden and

Jonathan stood facing each other in silence for several seconds. Jonathan eyed the blade in the warden's hand and knew that this was the end of it.

"LONG LIVE THE QUEEN!" Jonathan screamed as he ran with all his strength, fists raised, straight at the warden. The warden charged at Jonathan and raised the wicked sword above her head. In one swift stroke of the blade, it was over.

****

Hoops, Myra, and Doc ran through the tower, around several corners and down a few flights of stairs. They pushed open a wooden door and burst into an old storage room filled with wooden crates and barrels. On the far end of the room, behind a giant stack of crates, they found Chase. He stood in front of the tunnel entrance. His back was turned to them and he had a shovel in his hand.

"What happened!" demanded Myra. "Where's Jonathan?" She looked at the tunnel entrance and saw that it had been collapsed shut by the shovel in Chase's hand. "Chase! What have you done?!"

Chase slowly turned to face them. His eyes were black, inky orbs as Braxo spoke through them.

"There you are! Give it to me, Worthington. It's over." He stepped towards Hoops. *"Your friend is lost. You cannot escape. It's over. Now, GIVE IT TO ME!"*

Chase lurched at Hoops, but Doc stepped between them.

"Now hold on a minute, Chase. What in the world is…"

WHAM! With one violent punch, Chase sent the old man to the ground. His lip was cracked and bleeding. Myra tried to grab Chase's arm and stop him, but he easily tossed her small frame aside.

Hoops scrambled for the timepiece as he ran back towards the door. Chase was right behind him.

"You won't get away from me," Braxo's icy voice hissed, *"I'll always find you. It's MINE. Give me the timepiece!"*

Without looking, Hoops wound the pocket watch and rubbed. His hands and arms were stiff from fear, but he managed to summon the magic. Chase managed to grab the hem of Hoops' cloak, then his arm. As the glowing dust swirled around them both, Hoops clutched the timepiece with all his strength as Chase wrestled to grab his wrist.

Whoosh!

The Labyrinth

Crossing over to another world had no effect on Chase's determination to overpower Hoops and steal the timepiece. Braxo had full control of the teenager's body and was no stranger to magic.

Materializing on the sandstone floor, Hoops and Chase continued to wrestle, but Chase overpowered him. There wasn't a whole lot Hoops could do. He was only ten years old, fighting a young-adult man, and the two months of karate lessons he had taken a year ago would do nothing to help him fend off his enemy. So, Hoops wriggled and thrashed like a wild animal. He was afraid for his life, and he went wild. Chase had a hard time holding onto him, so he just kept a grip on the cloak with one hand while reaching for the timepiece with the other.

The black eyes still hummed with the anger and dark magic. "Give it to me. It belongs to me. You cannot escape." The eyes were terrifying up close. Hoops did everything he could to avoid looking at them.

Chase suddenly gripped the cloak with his other hand, this time at the collar just below Hoops' neck. The wild animal in Hoops ten-year-old brain went crazy. Hoops opened his mouth, tucked his chin, and bit into Chase's hand as hard as he could. He bit all the way down until his teeth scraped bone. He tightened his jaw to make his teeth come together, and they almost did.

Chase screamed and let go of the cloak, but Hoops didn't let up his assault. Crazed with fear, he clawed at the teenager's face like an eagle trying to sink its talons into a snake. His fingers plunged into the black eyes and he screamed at them in anger. Chase stumbled backward, his hand bleeding, and eyes shut. Hoops launched one last counterattack and kicked his leather boot between the teenager's legs with all his remaining strength. He knew his foot had found its target when Chase's body instantly dropped to the ground on his knees.

Hoops had only a moment to get away. Not knowing where he was, or caring which direction to go, he slipped the hood of his cloak over his head and ran for his life. He heard Braxo's enraged scream fill the air behind him.

Hoops ran down a hallway with no ceiling. The walls and floor were made of giant sandstone blocks. The walls were at least twenty feet high, offering no chance of climbing out. The hallway came to an end, allowing Hoops to go either left or right. He chose to go left, making a mental note of his turn. The end of this new hallway glowed from the light of what Hoops thought may be a portal—a shimmering green oval disc in the wall about five feet high. Looking back over his shoulder, he saw Chase round the corner, his black eyes glowing. Pulling the cloak close to him, Hoops pressed himself against the wall. Chase couldn't see the boy, neither could Braxo, so he spun around and slowly moved towards the other end of this hallway, to the right.

"I know you're here, boy. I know you still have it. Give it to me. I will never stop. I will always find you."

The opposite hallway, the one leading to the right, ended with a red portal embedded in the wall. Scouring the walls and floor for any sign of the invisible boy, Chase had made only a few steps towards the red portal, when a monstrous roar boomed into the hallway.

"TRESPASSER!"

Hoops was frozen with fear, but the bellowing voice didn't seem to affect Chase at all while Braxo had control of him.

Through the red glowing portal stepped an enormous creature. It had the body of a muscular man completely covered in black hair. But its feet were hooves, and it had the head of a terrifying bull. Broad leather straps crisscrossed its wide chest and connected to an equally wide belt. Its horns were black, sharp, and vicious. Hoops had read about this monster in a mythology book—a minotaur.

"TRESPASSER!" it bellowed again when its eyes fell on the teenager. When Chase turned to run from the beast, Hoops saw that his eyes no longer glowed black. Chase was himself again, and he was panicked, dazed, and beside himself with confusion and fear. His head turned this way and that, up and down, trying to make sense of his surroundings while his legs took him down the hallway towards the green portal. Hoops didn't move or reveal himself. He just watched. The minotaur charged at Chase and in four or five wide, easy strides, caught up to him. The thick, hairy hands seized the teenager and dragged him through the green portal. Hoops followed with his hood still over his head.

When he emerged from the portal, he watched the minotaur take a right at a junction up ahead. When Hoops got to the junction, he saw that the long hallway to the left ended with a white portal embedded in the wall. If he were to continue straight ahead, and not turn to the right or left, the hallway ended in a dazzling blue portal. But the creature took a right, so he followed. At the end of this hallway stood the minotaur. Chase couldn't free himself from its grip. The creature easily lifted the teenager with both arms and slung him into a slowly swirling black portal. Chase's scream suddenly stopped a moment later, after he had disappeared into the black void. Tiptoeing closer, Hoops could smell sulfur and rotting meat. He heard moans of agony and distant screams coming from the portal. He felt sick inside thinking of the suffering of the souls trapped inside. He imagined that hell must be something like this and he had no interest in learning more about what may await him through that black hole in the wall.

The minotaur turned around and slowly strode past the invisible boy, down the hall, and taking a right, slipped through the blue portal. Hoops softly ran after him, making as little noise as his leather boots would allow. Slipping through the blue portal, the world seemed to change.

He stepped out the other side onto a rocky, sandy ground. The night sky above was full of brilliant colorful stars, like what he had seen in Torpil. He counted five dazzling moons of differing sizes, each one dominating its own portion of the stellar dome above.

The minotaur was nowhere to be found, so Hoops slipped off the hood of the cloak to get a clearer view of the world around him, and the night sky. He stood in a desert plain. There were no mountains in the distance. There were no plants, trees, bugs, or animals. There was nothing but a desert stuck in time at night. The light from the heavens above illuminated the ground enough for Hoops to notice the hoof prints of the minotaur heading straight ahead away from the blue portal. Tracking the beast through the desert sand was easy, so he followed the prints for about a hundred yards to where they disappeared over the edge of a cliff. Hoops stood atop a black canyon. At least he thought it might be a canyon. He couldn't see the other side, or the bottom. It was too dark. There was just blackness. *This is what the edge of the world must be like.* But from the darkness below, he could hear the faint moans and screams that had frightened him at the black portal.

Stepping backwards away from the cliff's edge, a monstrous voice bellowed from behind him, "TRESPASSER!"

He spun around to see the minotaur stepping through the portal, eyes locked on the boy. The beast beat his hoof into the sand as only a bull can, then charged at Hoops with alarming speed. Hoops grabbed the edges of his hood and whisked it over his head. The bull-man slid to a stop, wildly panting, snot oozing from its nose. It turned this way and that, sniffing the air.

"I smell you, man-child," it growled.

As it followed Hoops' scent, it would take a slow step in his direction. Closer and closer with each step of his hoof. Hoops stepped to his right as lightly and quietly as he could to sneak around the beast, but the monster's nose was keen, and it still moved in Hoops' direction.

He knew he'd never make it around the minotaur if he ran for the portal now. Just then, he remembered he had the knife! He slipped it out of his belt and pointed its blue blade at the beast. Nothing. No vibration. No sensation in his stomach. He wouldn't be taking control of this magical creature's mind which made him think there must be something special about the minotaur. Still, he knew he was in great danger and as a last resort, he tiptoed back to the cliff's edge.

He slipped the hood off his head but didn't let go of the cloak.

"I'm over here, you stinky meat sack!" he shouted.

The beast jerked in his direction, bellowed and charged. Its arms were raised, and it had murder in its eyes.

Not yet. Hoops told himself. He allowed the distance between him and the mythical beast to close. His knees shook, and he thought that he must be crazy. Still, this was his only chance of escape.

Not yet. The creature moved faster and the closer it got, the more terrifying it looked. Only yards away, Hoops knew the moment was now or never.

NOW! He slipped the hood over his head and dropped to the ground just as the beast lunged at him. He grabbed his knees and curled up in a tight ball. There wasn't enough ground left for the bulky creature to slow down and turn, and it tumbled over the edge of the cliff. Its roar echoed up from the blackness as it fell further and further down. Eventually, he could no longer hear it, only the moans and screams from the lost souls below.

Removing the hood, Hoops walked back to the blue portal and stepped through. It was time to explore the secrets of the labyrinth.

Chamber of Crossroads

At the junction, where the two great sandstone hallways cross, Hoops decided to take a right and investigate the glowing white portal. He had witnessed the horrors of the black one, to the left. He had defeated the minotaur in the desert of the blue portal behind him and knew that the green option directly ahead took him to the split hallway and back to the beginning of the labyrinth. Approaching the swirling white disc, embedded in the wall, he pulled his knife out and stuck the tip of the blade through. Pulling it back, the knife was unaltered and whole. It now seemed safe to stick a body part through the portal. He thrust his hand through and pulled it back. Same thing, all whole. Taking a breath, he carefully stepped through with his whole body. To his disappointment, he stood at the entrance of the labyrinth again. On the ground, he could see scuff marks from where he and Chase had wrestled for the timepiece. Up ahead, the hallway split to the left, through the green portal, and to the right, where the red portal awaited. All that remained was that one. He had seen the minotaur emerge from that blood-red circle, when Chase was seized. Now that the creature was no longer a threat, Hoops felt it was time to explore.

The sky above the labyrinth walls seemed uneasy. It was disturbed with rolling grey clouds and distant thunder. Something was happening in the labyrinth. Anger filled the air. Hoops felt uncertain about continuing and stood before the red glowing gate, wondering if he should just move on to the next world. He had certainly had enough excitement in this one and wasn't interested in seeing more creatures or friends hurt. He pulled out his timepiece and, looking down, set it for eleven o'clock.

"TRESPASSER!" The minotaur jumped out of the great red circle and grabbed Hoops in an instant.

"Stop! Please! I'm trying to leave, just let me go!" Hoops was in shock.

The beast seemed deaf to Hoops' begging and walked through the green gate to the junction. Hoops panicked. He had dropped the pocket watch as the minotaur dragged him by the hood of his cloak. He knew his fate was to be tossed into that black, horrible void. Taking a right at the crossing of the hallways, the minotaur approached the black, stinking, moaning portal.

Reaching down to grab the boy with both of his black hairy hands, the creature wasn't prepared for the blue steel that sliced through his arm! Hoops had pulled the knife from his belt and slashed. Bellowing in pain, the minotaur released his grip and Hoops crawled backwards and jumped up to his feet. He yelled in fear as he swung the knife in front of him, slashing and waving the blade like the conductor of an orchestra. The sting of the knife's bite was enough to give the beast a second thought before lunging at him again. Hoops had enough time to pull his hood over his head. As the beast swung its mighty palm at the invisible boy, Hoops dropped to the ground and slipped between its legs. With his back to the dark portal and the minotaur's hairy back in front of him, Hoops put both hands around the knife's handle and stabbed it deep into the back of the bull-man's neck. The creature reached back with both arms in agony, trying to grasp the penetrating blade. His angry and pain-filled cries thundered through the junction. Hoops circled around in front of the beast, and without losing a second, he kicked as hard as he could. The minotaur stumbled backwards, tripping over its own hooves, and dazed from the knife attack. Rocking back, the beast fell to the ground like a great tree. His bulky body landed flat on its back... but the head of the beast went through the swirling black portal.

It was a gruesome sight: the headless body of the minotaur lying dead on the ground, a pool of dark reddish-brown blood pooling around the gaping hole in the top of its neck. Thunder pealed and lightning flashed in disapproval above. The labyrinth was unhappy with the death of its champion.

Suddenly, it occurred to Hoops that the knife had fallen through the black portal along with the beast's head. It was lost, and there was no way Hoops was going in after it. Instead, he headed back to the beginning of the labyrinth where he could safely use the timepiece without any strange thing coming out of any strange portal. As he stepped through the green gate on his way back, he was shocked to see the head of the great black minotaur squeezing out of the oozing red portal ahead. The bull's head fell to the ground and onto its side, the knife still lodged in the back of its neck. When it landed, one of the eyes popped out and dangled from its socket. The rest of the beast didn't emerge. Only the head had been regenerated... but it was alive.

"TRESPASSER!" it yelled at Hoops. But it simply lay there on the ground. Hoops calmly walked over and pulled the knife from its neck, then picked up the head by one of its horns. He had to use both hands.

Lifting it up to eye level, the beast spoke, "Restore me, man-child. You don't know what you've done." As he spoke, more thunder shook the sky above.

Hoops was tired of being scared, "NO. We need to talk. You're coming with me." He pulled out the timepiece and set it for six thirty. This time, the pocket watch didn't reset itself, and Hoops felt a flood of relief knowing that he'd be home in a few short moments. He wound and rubbed the timepiece with his left hand, while the horned head of the minotaur dangled in his right. The cyclone of electricity swished around him. *What am I going to tell Mom when she sees this thing?*

Whoosh!

What a sight it must've been to see a boy with a magic cloak and leather boots suddenly materialize in the living room, holding the head of a talking bull. Hoops was sure that his mom would faint, and he was fully prepared to call 911. But Mom wasn't there. It was the middle of the afternoon, and the apartment was empty. He felt like he'd been gone for years, and the room was hazy with memories. But this was his home. He was back.

"Take me back, traveler. You don't know what you've done," grunted the bull.

"You're not going anywhere until you give me some answers," Hoops snapped at the beast. "Who are you?"

"I am Sentinel. I am the guardian of the labyrinth, and the keeper of the secret."

"What secret?" Hoops demanded.

"Dumb question, man-child," the bull snorted. "None shall enter. None shall escape."

"Well, I guess you'll be staying here with me until you tell me more, Sentinel. And it's going to be hard to guard your labyrinth and your secret without your body. So, until you tell me what I want to know, you're stuck here with me."

The minotaur was quiet for a long time. Hoops set him on the floor and sat cross legged in front of him. They were eye to eye, locked in a staring contest. Hoops was great at that game and would get his answers.

"Sentinel, if you want me to return you to the labyrinth, you're going to have to tell me the secret."

"No. You don't know what you've done, boy." The minotaur moaned.

"What is the labyrinth hiding?"

"The chamber," said the beast. "It contains the secret. It must not be found. All trespassers seek it. NO trespassers must find it. None shall enter. None shall escape."

"The chamber, huh?" Hoops was curious enough to *almost* want to go back. "So, where is this chamber? I looked all over the labyrinth, went through every portal. It's just hallways and gates. It's not even that big."

Sentinel grunted, "Only I can enter. The door is hidden. None shall enter. None..."

"...shall escape," Hoops interrupted. "Blah, blah, blah. I get it. Where is the door hidden?"

The minotaur said nothing.

"Where is the door hidden, Sentinel?" Hoops was growing annoyed with this bull-headed grump.

"Foolish child! The labyrinth lies wide open to trespassers because of you!" the beast scolded. "I keep the secret. I keep THEM locked up. I keep the world from their chaos. I am the guardian. They must not escape. Trespassers seek the secret, the chamber, but THEY await to be released. THEY will destroy the worlds. Now, no one watches. No one guards. No one keeps the secret safe. Foolish boy. Your selfish thirsting for adventure has led the worlds to the edge of chaos and evil. Take me back, boy."

Hoops saw that he had made a mistake. This wasn't an evil beast. He was created to guard something very important. Hoops felt like he had just discovered the world's rarest, most precious flower and plucked it from its stem for his own pleasure.

"Okay, Sentinel. Here's what's going to happen. I'll take you back. But I won't restore you until you show me this chamber."

"If I show you the chamber, you'll restore me. If you restore me, I'll expel you. You may die, boy."

"You'll show me the chamber, then I'll restore you. I'll be gone before you can catch me, though." Hoops gripped the timepiece. He was a little worried about the plan, but Sentinel gave him answers and he wanted to see this 'secret.'

The beast said, "Make an oath. You WILL restore me."

"I promise."

Hoops grabbed the timepiece, resetting it for ten o'clock. He grabbed one of Sentinel's great horns as the swirl tightened around them.

Whoosh!

"Forward," Sentinel directed. They started in a new hallway. Or maybe it was the same hallway. Hoops wasn't sure. Everything was different. There were new junctions and portals. Nothing was familiar at all. The labyrinth had rearranged itself. Hoops asked Sentinel where they were.

"Labyrinth protects itself each time a trespasser arrives. You are the first to return. None shall enter. None shall return," he grumbled. "Stop here."

They stood at a dead end. The sandstone hallway just, well, ended.

"Push," ordered Sentinel. Hoops placed his hand on the sandstone wall and leaned into it. The sandstone bricks unlocked themselves and double doors swung open and inward. "Enter. But touch NOTHING," he growled.

"Enough with your dumb rules," Hoops complained as he walked into the chamber and gave his eyes time to adjust to the low light. It was a giant dome. The walls around the circular chamber were twenty feet high before curving into a stone hemisphere. All around the walls of the room were twelve portals. Each one glowed with a different color, and each was equally distanced from the next. Hoops walked alongside the wall, investigating each one. Etched in the stone floor before every portal was a different number.

"Are these the same twelve worlds of my timepiece?" he asked.

"This is the Chamber of Crossroads. Where one may pass from one world to another. This is the center," Sentinel offered. "The secret is there. In the middle."

Hoops turned and looked to the center of the great domed room and dazzling green crystal hovered twenty feet above. Its light illuminated the floor below and it pulsed slowly. He tried to act like he wasn't that impressed. "What's so special about that green rock?"

"Foolish man-child. That is the key. It keeps open the gates to all the worlds. And it keeps THEM locked away in darkness."

"You keep saying THEM and THEY. Who are you talking about?"

"Look above you. At the top of the chamber, boy."

Hoops looked upward into the dark, distant top of the dome. Embedded in the ceiling, at its very center was a black circle. It swirled with turbulent shadow, like black mist caught in a whirlpool. It was full of more cries and moans.

"What is that?!" Hoops hissed in fear.

"That is the prison. That is where THEY are locked up. None shall enter. None shall escape."

Hoops understood now. Sentinel protected the key to the worlds and was responsible for keeping that terrible darkness from being unleashed into the chamber. It made sense that Sentinel would trust no one, whether they were a traveler or not. The risk of anyone entering this chamber was too great and Hoops knew Sentinel had the most important mission of all: To trust no one and protect the secret. The thought of someone like Braxo entering the chamber and wielding his magic made him shudder. *He could rule all the worlds... or destroy them.*

"You made an oath, traveler," Sentinel reminded him.

"I did. And I'll keep it. Let's go." Hoops left the chamber with the head of Sentinel and was directed around corners and down hallways, until he lost track of where he might be in the labyrinth. Rounding one last turn, they came to a black portal with the headless body of the minotaur lying in front of it.

"Now, restore me," Sentinel ordered.

Hoops set his bull head down respectfully and used all his strength to push the heavy bulk of the minotaur's headless body through the portal. When he was done, he picked up Sentinel's head and looked him in the eye.

"I'm sorry. I didn't understand. Thank you for showing me the chamber." Hoops paused, then chanted, "None shall enter. None shall escape."

He tossed the head into the black gate, and quickly pulled out the timepiece. He rushed to set it to eleven o'clock, knowing what was about to happen. Rubbing the timepiece, he heard a monstrous bellow behind him.

"TRESPASSER!" Sentinel, fully regenerated, charged around a distant corner to do his job. Hoops smiled and was glad to see the guardian restored.

Whoosh!

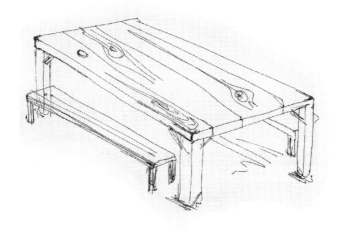

Traveler's Rest

The room erupted with shouts and cheers. A crowd of boys clapped and whooped and hollered. They were all looking at Hoops with beaming smiles splitting their faces. When Hoops appeared in the room just seconds ago, he stood on a circular wooden platform, raised only a foot or so above the floor. The room itself was about the size of his apartment back home, only there were no doors, windows, partitions, or other rooms walled off within. It was just one big room. The ceiling was low, about eight feet high or so, maybe ten. The floor and walls were made of rough wooden planks, as was the ceiling above. It was an enormous club house. On the far wall, opposite the platform he stood on, a broad yellow curtain hung. In bold red, the letters T and L were embroidered in wide capitals.

The cheers and clapping went on for some time until a tall, skinny boy with red hair, pushed his way to the front. He raised his hand to the boys behind him and the crowd hushed. With his back to Hoops, he addressed the crowd:

"Travelers, thank you for making it on such short notice. Today, we celebrate the arrival of Worthington D. Hooper, who has made it through the Four Gates and Five Worlds of the timepiece." The boys whooped and clapped at this. Hoops felt a little embarrassed with all eyes fixed on him. The redheaded boy continued his speech, "As you know, there have been many that didn't make it. Some were devoured. Some were drowned. Some had accidents, while others were captured and executed. Some were caught in the labyrinth and thrown into darkness, and many just plain-old quit." The room dead quiet. "But today arrives a boy who survived, who pushed through. Today arrives a brave kid, like you, who has earned his seat in this clubhouse of heroes." As the speech maker finished all this up, he turned around and faced Hoops. Looking him in the eye, he continued addressing the crowd. "This boy is worthy of our friendship. So, I hereby nominate Hoops to become a member of the Traveler's League."

It was Smitty! The boy who had first given him the timepiece and the scroll. It seemed like it was months ago. So much had happened since. So much had changed.

"Any opposed?" Smitty continued. The room remained still for several seconds, then with a smile, Smitty shouted, "ALL IN FAVOR?"

"AYE!" shouted every boy at once, before bursting into a ruckus of cheers and happy hollers.

Smitty motioned for Hoops to come down off the platform and led him to one of several long tables flanked by benches. They reminded him of the tables in the prison dining hall where he first met Myra, Doc, Jonathan, and Chase. *Poor Chase.* As he followed Smitty through the crowd of boys, many of them would pat him on the back or shoulder. Each one would say, "Great job," or "Well done," or "Welcome back." A few of them even grabbed Hoops' hand and shook it, saying, "Welcome to the league," or "Congratulations."

Smitty sat across from Hoops and a gang of younger boys immediately surrounded them, plopping down on the benches and leaning in close. Each one of the boys at the table wore the same gold medal dangling from a red and white-striped ribbon. Smitty's was different now. His medal had wings on each side.

"These are our best travelers, Hoops. Let me introduce you. This is Will. And that's Aiden. Over there is Thomas, Gavin, and Harry. Sitting next to you is Eli, and that's Toby on your right."

Toby was an older boy, maybe thirteen or fourteen. He was bigger than the others and had jet-black hair that swooped across the left side of his face.

"Sup?" he said, nodding his head back.

Smitty continued, "Toby is our *Retriever*. When a boy gives up, or doesn't make it through, Toby here is Special Ops. He goes in and retrieves the timepiece. And standing behind me is my wingman, Christian."

Christian was the tallest eight-year-old Hoops had ever seen. He had golden hair, blue eyes, and the look of serious genius all over his face.

"And this is Eli," Smitty continued. "He's the *Keeper*. He keeps this place clean and organized and makes sure all the travelers get the supplies they need."

"I also write down everyone's stories. We have a library of journals, full of all the details from every one of these guys' travels," Eli added.

Smitty continued, "And my name is..."

"Smitty!" Hoops said, smiling.

"That's *Captain* Smitty to you, newbie." Christian's head popped out from behind Smitty's right elbow. The whole gang laughed.

Eli handed a small box to Smitty, who pooped open the lid. He carefully pulled out a gold medal hanging from a red and white-striped ribbon and handed it to Hoops.

"This is yours now. You're one of us. Welcome to the Traveler's League."

Hoops carefully pinned the medal on his tunic, just above where a pocket would be on a normal boy's shirt.

"So... you've *all* used the timepiece?" Hoops was a little surprised.

"That's right. We've all traveled through every world with that pocket watch. Some of us have even made more than one trip. Like Toby. He knows about every detail of every world. A real veteran."

Toby smirked with the half of his face that wasn't covered in swooshing black hair. "I hate it when they don't make it through the ocean of Isango. Every time it's the same. Dive down to the crater and get the watch before the squid-shark sees me."

Hoops was a little embarrassed thinking that he was the first to discover that creature. "You mean the red cracken dobber?"

The boys all laughed, and Harry said, "That's the best name yet! We all just called it a squid-shark."

Hoops was sorry to break the news. "Yeah, I kinda, well… It was after me and I was trapped. And it had that weird sac thingy, all full of chemicals, and… I, uh, farted… and it, well… it died. I killed it."

The boys were silent. Stunned, with eyes the size of baseballs, someone said, "You actually killed squid-shark?"

"Yeah."

"Now," Smitty interrupted, "we *really* want to hear about your travels!"

Eli pulled out a journal and pen and scribbled like mad. "Start with one o'clock."

Hoops spent hours going from world to world, retelling every action and thought, every word and tiny thing he observed. Occasionally, he would skip something, like when he was crying in Torpil, or locked in the prison of Hapis, sobbing and singing to himself. When he told them about the Oracle, he decided it was better NOT to mention that the next traveler was supposed to be a girl. Come to think of it, there wasn't a single girl in the Traveler's League, none that he had seen anyway. But he felt as though he needed to tell Smitty. When the time was right, he'd do it.

As he romped through his adventurous account, the boys would excitedly shout questions at him, or sometimes interrupt him with a story of their own. Hoops had found friends. These were boys who loved the adventure, the danger, and the stories of bravery and close calls. He finally found a group of friends that made him feel like he belonged. He was a member of the Traveler's League now and had a group of friends that 'got him.' And to Hoops, that was more valuable than the timepiece itself.

"Wow," Smitty muttered when Hoops had finished. "That was the craziest adventure I've heard yet!" All the boys agreed that Hoops had a one-of-a-kind journey. "And I'm pretty sure you're the only traveler to have defeated Sentinel. Everyone else just runs away. You're the only boy to have gotten Sentinel to show you the chamber. We've all seen the chamber, of course, but none of us have tricked Sentinel the way you did."

"You've seen the Chamber of Crossroads?" Hoops asked.

"How do you think I retrieve the timepiece?" Toby smirked again. "Aiden, pull the curtain."

Aiden was nine, rail thin, and short, but he was the fastest kid in the Traveler's League. He jumped up, ran to the big yellow curtain and pulled a rope that hung on one side. As the pulley turned, the yellow fabric slid back, slowly uncovering a glowing white disc embedded in the wall. The light swirled around inside it like a cloud caught in a cyclone.

"A portal?!" Hoops jumped up.

"Not just any portal, Hoops. This takes you straight into the Chamber. From there, as you know, you can travel anywhere."

"There's a portal hidden in every world," Christian added, "and it's our job to make sure Braxo doesn't know about it. If he found the portal hidden in Sirihbaz, he wouldn't need the timepiece. He would invade all the worlds."

"We'd stop him." Thomas was quiet but bubbled with an angry energy. Hoops knew right away he was the toughest kid in the room.

Aiden pulled the curtain back over the portal and returned to the table. Eli stood and dug through some wooden boxes he had piled up in the corner. Smitty and Gavin checked out Hoops' dagger.

"Smitty?" Hoops needed to talk to him about what the Oracle said. "You got a second to talk... *alone?*" Gavin was distracted with the dagger, so Smitty stood and walked with Hoops to an empty corner of the clubhouse.

"What is it?"

"The Oracle told me," Hoops looked over his shoulder to make sure no one else was listening, "that a *girl* was the only one who could save Sirihbaz."

"So what?"

"The Oracle said that a girl would be... the next traveler."

Smitty was quiet for a minute. "That's not good. The League won't like that at all. There hasn't been a girl traveler in like, forty years. Ever since that one girl left that kid behind in Sirihbaz, we've only had boys using the timepiece."

"But when you first met me, you said that the timepiece chose me. Why hasn't the timepiece chosen any girls in so long?"

"I don't know." Smitty looked worried and annoyed. "But a girl can't be a member of the Traveler's League. It's boys only. It's called the 'Old Rule.' After that first girl goofed things up so badly, the League voted that no girls would be allowed to join. Ever."

Hoops thought that was a stupid rule. Not because he liked girls or cared about being fair. He just wanted to save his friends, and the Oracle had been crystal clear; only a girl could defeat Braxo and save Sirihbaz.

"Can't you just make a vote and change the Old Rule?"

Smitty huffed, "And go down in history as the *worst* captain ever? You're crazy if you think I'll let that happen. I've got a job to do here, Hoops. This is serious."

And saving the world of Sirihbaz isn't? Hoops didn't say it though. He only thought it. He knew it was pointless to continue talking about it with Smitty.

"Anyway, don't worry about that right now." Smitty loosened up a little bit and smiled. "You're not done traveling, you know? You still have one more trip to make."

Hoops had totally forgotten about using the timepiece again. Being with his new friends and a part of the Traveler's League was the best thing that had happened to him since this whole adventure began. He had lost track of time. He hadn't thought about home, or his mom, or the fact there was one last travel to make.

"Right. I guess I should finish. Where am I going?"

Smitty said, "It's your first official mission as a member of the Traveler's League. And it's also your last mission."

Eli walked up to them and handed Hoops a bundle of clothes, some tennis shoes, and an empty backpack.

"Here. Put these on. You can use the backpack to put your cloak, tunic, and other stuff in."

Hoops unfolded a pair of blue jeans, a collared shirt, and some socks. He would wear *normal* clothes again. He quickly changed and filled his backpack with the gifts WolliTom had given him. When he was done, he looked like any other kid on his way home from school, except for the gold medal dangling from the red and white-striped ribbon. It was pinned above his left shirt pocket.

"You'll need this." Smitty handed him a rolled-up piece of paper sealed with a blob of red wax.

A feeling of loneliness crawled all over him. He looked at Smitty and sheepishly said, "So, will I ever get to come back?"

"Of course!" laughed Smitty. "Don't be so dramatic. You'll be summoned when the *next* traveler arrives, or we have some special emergency meeting. We'll talk more then."

They led Hoops back to the round platform. He stepped up, pulled the pocket watch out, and set it for twelve o'clock. Rubbing the lid for the last time, he turned and looked over the crowd of faces. The faces of heroes and adventurers. The faces of his friends.

The Last Mission

The gushing of water, the warmth of the early summer sunshine, and the cooing of pigeons worked in unison to wake Hoops from what felt like a hard nap. His head felt like it was full of fog and he had a hard time getting and keeping his eyes open. Sitting up, the side of his neck ached. His head had been tilted as he had slept curled up on his side. He guessed he had been out for several hours at least and backpacks didn't make great pillows. For that matter, park benches didn't make great beds, not even his favorite one.

As his head cleared, his surroundings made sense. This was his park, the one in front of his apartment building. This was the park he crossed on his way home from school with his friends. And this was the very center of the park. The large fountain gushed and gurgled, and flights of pigeons would come and go, looking for whatever they could scrounge, scrape, or steal from clumsy, crumb-dropping humans.

Everything seemed so normal and familiar. It was like he awoke in one of a thousand boring memories. But Hoops was okay with being bored for a change. It was nice to not wake in danger. There were no bears, toxigators, marsh trolls, or minotaurs anywhere around. The sunshine felt like a warm 'welcome home' hug, and the entire summer break remained unplanned before him. He was so glad to be back.

For a moment, he wondered if all his adventures with the timepiece had just been one long, tiring dream. *Did I fall asleep on my way home from school?* He unzipped the backpack laying next to him and peeked inside to find animal-skin clothes, a cloak, and leather boots. His heart beat faster, and he jumped up and stuck his hands in his pockets. The pocket watch was in his right pocket and it was set for twelve o'clock, and a small scroll of paper was in his left. His heart raced now. He rubbed his hand on his shirt and felt the cool medal and smooth fabric of the ribbon pinned above his left pocket. This was no dream. He was home, but he wasn't done. His last mission had brought him to his own world, and not only that, it had brought him to the park right in front of his home!

"Let's get this over with, Hoops" he told himself.

He had no idea what to do, or what would happen. He didn't know what his last mission was. He just knew the timepiece had a way of taking him to the right starting place to begin whatever his next adventure might be. So, he just walked. Hoops had walked on every path in this park hundreds of times before. He could visualize a perfectly accurate map in his head and get from one end to the other blindfolded. He was so familiar with the park, he would end up walking home out of habit. His body just knew how to get home without thinking, and would turn here or there, and he would jump over cracks and steps while his mind worked on other more important things.

Then he froze.

He couldn't make any sense of what lay on the ground in front of him. He squeezed his eyes shut, and opened them, but it was still there. He did it again, same thing. Rubbing his eyes and pinching himself didn't make it change. He closed his eyes tight one last time, took a deep breath, and opened them. It was still there. They BOTH were. Hoops looked at two shadows shooting out from his feet. The bright sun was on his back, but it made two equally black shadows, but the one on the right was very strange. It had its shadowy arm raised, finger pointing down a split in the pathway that led to a playground. Hoops walked straight ahead and past the split, but the shadow kept pointing in the direction of the playground. No matter which direction he walked, or where in the park he found himself, his extra shadow kept its finger pointed the same way. Just like a compass remained pointing north as he turned or spun his body, the shadow didn't shift at all.

Hoops gave in. He followed the direction of his shadowy guide and headed down the path for the playground. A few small kids tumbled, tripped, and trampled on the jungle gym. As he passed under the shade of trees along the path, his shadows would disappear, but always returned with the one on the right guiding him forward. He found an empty bench and sat, watching and waiting for whatever would happen next.

After a while, some of the parents moved on to other activities in the park, prying their whining toddlers and crying babies away from the metal kiddy kingdom. New parents and kids would arrive and replace them, and it would all start over. Every so often, a kid about Hoops' age would ride his bike or skateboard past the playground.

Hoops wondered how long he would have to sit and wait for something to happen, when finally, a boy about ten years old rode up on his bike. It plopped over on its side as the kid jumped off and climbed to the top of the jungle gym. He looked like the king of the monkeys showing off how quickly he could get up there.

As he watched the kid climb and play, he had this weird feeling. The timepiece felt like it was vibrating or buzzing in his pocket. He pulled it out and looked it over. Suddenly, he realized his travels were over and his last mission was to give the pocket watch away. He stood slowly and walked towards the jungle gym. The boy at the top, about his age, was busy swinging and balancing, towering above all the smaller kids, like a tall, bored veteran.

Movement out of the corner of Hoops' eye made him glance towards the ground. The second shadow was pointing away from the jungle gym towards the swing set. All the swings were empty except one. A girl a year or two younger than Hoops pumped the swing to its highest. Her gold-red ponytail would wave like a flag when she'd swoosh upward, and she had a look on her face that she was determined to make her swing go upside down this time. Looking back down, the second shadow's finger pointed directly at the girl. *Oh no! Smitty said no girls. The Old Rule! He'll be furious. I can't. I'm a member of the Traveler's League, now. I must follow the rules. They're my friends. It's the Old Rule!* His mind made every reason and excuse to not follow the shadow's direction.

He turned back towards the boy, dead set on delivering the gifts to him. But the Oracle's words echoed in his mind. *You must finish your travels. Only then can the girl be found. Only then can your friends be saved.* He remembered the kindness of his first friends, WolliTom and Dewin. He remembered the cruel and wicked Braxo, and the terror and pain he caused. *Only SHE can stop him,* the Oracle had told him.

Staring at the boy, Hoops knew what must be done. He knew what was right, and though he was scared to do it, he also knew that bravery didn't come without fear.

"It's a stupid rule anyway," he told himself as he turned back and followed the shadow to the swinging girl.

When he got to the swing set, the girl noticed him, and made a dazzling leap from the swing's highest point. A perfect landing made Hoops a little jealous.

"Awesome!" he said.

"Thanks," the girl chirped. "I've been practicing."

"I know this sounds weird, but I've been looking all over this park for you. I have something for you..."

"Who are you?" the girl replied. "Do you go to my school or something?"

"No. You don't know me, but I know who you are. Well, kind of. I know who you *will* be," Hoops smiled as he talked. "My name's Worthington Hooper... friends call me 'Hoops.'" He extended his hand for a handshake, and as he did, the girl noticed a gold medal hanging from a red and white-striped ribbon. It was pinned to his shirt just above his left pocket.

Out of his pocket, he pulled a small rolled-up piece of paper like a scroll, tied with a red ribbon and sealed with a blob of red wax. The wax seal had the letters "T.L." stamped on it. Hoops handed the scroll to the girl.

"Don't break the seal and read the scroll until you get home," he said.

"Okaaaay. Weird. What is it? A birthday invitation or something?"

Hoops smiled again. "It's the code. The Traveler's Code."

"All right. Well, thanks for the weird note." The girl turned to walk away.

"Wait! I haven't given you the rest of it," Hoops shouted after her. "This is the best part!"

He reached in his *other* pocket and pulled out the old pocket watch. He opened it and set it to one o'clock and handed it to her.

"Don't wind it up until you get home. And read the Traveler's Code first."

She reached out slowly and took the timepiece, looking it over with great care.

"My name's Eva Mae." She tried to be polite but at the same time, figure out why she was being given a gift by a strange boy. "So... you're just giving it to me? Why?"

"Because I have to. It's my last mission." Hoops looked a little sad. "And it's chosen you to be next."

"Next?" Eva Mae was confused, and curious all at once. "The next *WHAT*?" she said as she looked down at the timepiece in her hand.

"You're the next traveler!" said Hoops.

A thousand questions raced through her eight-year-old brain, but when she looked up, Hoops was *gone*.

The End

Note from the Author

NICHOLAS GOSS has been a piano teacher, sailboat builder, private investigator, barista, and salesman. He has a collection of more books than he could possibly read in his lifetime and lives with his head firmly stuck in the clouds. He resides in Nashville with his wife, two kids, and their labradoodle, Shelby. His host of eccentric hobbies include woodworking, sailing, fencing, ping pong, hammocking, and playing the penny whistle. Can you imagine what his neighbors must think?

Yeah. You guessed it: he was homeschooled.

The Traveler's League Book Series was born when he strayed from the normal bedtime routine of reading, and instead created new worlds full of funny characters, action, magic, and adventure. Since then, he has committed himself to entertaining children through writing books that make kids feel the magic of adventure and friendship. All the books in the series are available on Amazon.

Made in the USA
Monee, IL
23 November 2019